Joseph Hone was born in 1937
He was a producer with
UN Secretariat in New
has since been living in
broadcasts frequently on
current affairs. His first n
published in 1971, and this
Sixth Directorate. A collecti and autobiograph-
ical essays, *The Dancing Waiters*, was also published in
1975.

Here, in *Irish Ghost Stories*, he has brought together
ten ghost stories specially written by ten of Ireland's best
contemporary writers in a collection that is genuinely
disturbing and compulsively readable.

Irish Ghost Stories

specially written by

Robert Bernen – Tom Crowe
Desmond Hogan – Joseph Hone
Jennifer Johnston – John McGahern
Brian Moore – Peter Somerville-Large
William Trevor – Terence de Vere White

edited by
Joseph Hone

GRAFTON BOOKS
A Division of the Collins Publishing Group

LONDON GLASGOW
TORONTO SYDNEY AUCKLAND

Grafton Books
A Division of the Collins Publishing Group
8 Grafton Street, London W1X 3LA

Published by Granada Publishing Limited
in Panther Books 1979
Reprinted 1990

First published in Great Britain by
Hamish Hamilton Ltd 1977

ISBN 0-586-04603-8

Printed and bound in Great Britain by
Collins, Glasgow

Set in Times

Contents

ROBERT BERNEN

Brock

'A small brown dog, the colour of a badger. And you would hear no voice from him. Nor the sheep would not scare before him, the way they will before a black dog, when he was so like the badger, you see, for they'll not scare before the badger neither.'

Paddy Rua's kitchen was a mass of irregular stone wall, built long before mortar or plaster was known in the Donegal hills, but smoothed to gentle undulations by generations of whitewash, topped above by the arch of crude roof, the rough-hewn timbers and wattles softened and darkened by equally long generations of smoke from the low stone hearth. The storms that warned of their approach by sending the smoke adversely down the stone chimney to fill the low kitchen had coated the wood with a dark, oily soot and so preserved it from worm and rot. Some thought the soot had preserved the people of the house too with its penetrating astringency, and Paddy Rua, somewhere in his nineties, could still rise from his stool beside the hearth to go out the kitchen door and look over his land and as much of his hill as could be seen, in the ancient manner of farmers scanning the ground to satisfy himself that all was in order, that cattle and sheep were grazing in their accustomed manner and haunts, and that 'nothing strange' had interrupted the normal, safe course of animal life on his land. But mostly he sat close to his hearth and its piled turf, turning first one side and then the other to the glowing heat, and recollecting a time before any trace of modern life had been felt in the hills. By agreement Paddy Rua was in his nineties, though some thought he was near the beginning of them, while others put him well further on. A young valley farmer, careless of the nice discretion of the hills, had asked him, and Paddy Rua had thought for a while before speaking.

'Damned if I can mind.'

He looked at the fire.

'Damned if I can mind it now. It be to be in the parish register, for Father Cleary there, God rest him, he was there that time, and he looked it out. That was the time the pensions first come to this country, and he looked it out to see when was I baptized and was I the age for the pension. But damned if I can mind what year ago that were.'

A long discussion followed, with ample intervals for recollection and consideration, between Paddy Rua, sitting by the hearth, and his wife Mary, a generation younger and ceaselessly shuffling back and forth between hearth and kitchen table as she put bread on to roast above the fire or added fresh water to the kettle or, for want of other work, simply swept the red ashes of the burnt turf back into the hearth, tirelessly interjecting brief affirmative commentaries on Paddy's words – 'Aye, caddy, you're right there,' was the usual formula, for even at Paddy's great age she still called him 'caddy' in sign of approval and affection – and their son Briney Paddy Rua, another generation younger still, the real 'caddy' of the house, the human power source for any heavy work. Their voices contrasted by turns, the sound of the wind in Paddy's but the mist and rain in his son's, and in his wife's throat the thin twitter of a bird. But the only conclusion of their deliberations was that 'it be to be twenty year or more since the pensions come out first', and nothing more was said about Paddy Rua's age. One thing only was certain, and that was that every trace of the fiery redness of hair that had given Paddy Rua his name had yielded to a perfect, silvery white.

'Aye,' he said, going back to his recollection of the brown dog. '*Het* was a bad winter, you would say, when the snow lay about the streets in wreathes for months and weren't gone from the hills until summer. By Christ the sheep got it hard that year. There was ones lost in the snow in the high hills beyont, and not got at all until spring, and then only the horns got, and bits of fleece. And there would be more lost too, oh loads more, only a man had a good dog to take them to him.' To which remark there were more affirmations, both from the wife and the son, who simply shook his downcast head slowly and commented, 'Oh, aye, indeed, you want a good dog with the sheep.'

A glowing turf on the hearth dislodged itself from the rest of the fire and tumbled on to the flagstones at Paddy's feet. He took up the black iron tongs that stood propped in a corner of the hearth near him and began a delicate rearrangement of the brick-like chunks of turf, until the integrity of the fire had been restored. Then he rose and went to the door, and looked up towards the hills.

'There's a name on every part of the hill. A name in Irish, that a man would know where he was, and if he saw a sheep lost there, or something else like that, he could tell the man that lost it, and him go straight to where it were, and take it with him.'

He stood on the 'street', as he called the level clay ground before his house, and looked over the land before him.

'That hill there now, away from us there, *Cruk Mian* we call that, the Fine Hill. And that big rock you see, that's *Caricka Keena*, the Rock of the Fog, the green fog that grows about the hills. And the high hill there beyont the river, that's *Ben Bwee*, the Yellow Hill. And there above, above the path that we go out and in, that's *Ben Doo*, is the name that's on it in Irish, and in English they call it the Black Spink. *Het's* the bad article.'

He looked upwards along the steeply sloping green hill that rose behind his house to the uneven mass of vertical black rock that capped it. High, dark, irregular, a looming shadow of rock crossed by strips of green that attracted sheep and drew them, at times when grass was scarce, by gradual degrees further and further in to the sharp, uneven cliff face, until they found themselves isolated, marooned on a narrow ledge of rock with no way out, none at least that they could find. One who knew sheep could perceive, even from the river-valley five hundred feet below, their near-sighted perplexity as they stood, shifting their stance only intermittently, waiting as though in patient expectation of an opening to appear, of further grazing before them to lead them on, then returning to an examination of the scanty well-picked sward under their feet – but mostly simply standing, expectant, patient.

It happened two or three times a year, this catching of sheep in a natural trap. Almost always it was the year-old ewes – the 'yirrols' – that got caught, sheep in the first part of their lives that had not yet learned to be sufficiently wary. And then the sheep farmers looked upwards from the river valley, calm, betraying no anguish or sense of loss. That was felt inwardly, not expressed. To count the loss aloud would only be to add discouragement to damage. But mostly it was hard, or impossible, to get the sheep out again.

'Excepting a man had a good dog could take them out of it,' Briney Paddy Rua said over his shoulder as he sat at the small wooden table in the far corner of the kitchen, facing the wall and taking his bread and tea. Above him, in the spaces between the wattles and the earth sods of the roof itself tobacco-darkened clay pipes were wedged, and two pairs of wool-shears hung from wooden pegs, their points downwards. On the floor near the table stood a tall, unpainted wooden churn. Pinned to the wattles of the roof above the hearth was a Brigid cross woven of green rushes. Briney filled his mouth with bread, tearing it off with a sideways forceful motion of his head, and took a sip of tea.

'That brown dog now,' he said, 'he would take a sheep out of the spink, and do it handy. You would see him handle them quiet, very quiet. You would enjoy to see him do it.'

Paddy Rua looked over at his son for a moment.

'Did you know that dog?' he asked. 'I thought that dog was before your time. By God, I was only a young caddy myself when I had that dog, younger nor you are now, I doubt.'

Briney finished eating his mouthful.

'Well, I didn't know him,' he said. 'But I often hear tell, you see.'

'Aye,' Paddy resumed. '*Het* was a dog. Brock. That's the Irish on *badger*. You see, when he was so like the badger, we called Brock on him. And he was very biddable, and quiet. It was the nature of the dog, you see, that he would come when you whistle him and walk quiet at your foot. Nor he would not catch any sheep neither, nor do them no harm.'

'He was a great dog indeed,' Mary interjected, twittering as she poured more tea from an old aluminium teapot into Briney's cup. 'Aye, caddy, he was a good one.'

'Thon was the dog could take the yirrols from the spink,' Briney added.

'He could!' Paddy Rua said with emphasis, his eyes beginning to glow with the evoked past.

'By God, there are plenty of good dogs now can do

nothing in the spink,' Briney went on. 'For there is Charley Fetey's big yellow dog that's as good as any dog these parts, would take the sheep to you as nicely' – Briney smiled and held his arm in a gentle, horizontal arc before him – 'and put them in the yard for you, and you doing nothing only standing looking on. But if the same dog would come to the spink, you would have work to get him out, you would have to carry him out of it yourself, for he can do nothing in it, only stand. He would be afeared, you see.'

'Aye,' Paddy said. 'I often seen that. But the brown dog was afeared of nothing, and would go in along them wee ledges, and as quiet' – he gestured tranquillity with his hands – 'and turn the sheep, the way they would make their way out again, quiet, very quiet. Many's the sheep he took out of that Black Spink. And in that bad winter when the snow lay about the streets in wreathes until spring he was in it four or five times – he was! – and he saved a pile of sheep. You would see the wee brown dog that clear on the white snow. Back and forth, back and forth, until the sheep was out. Sheep that were in it and would be starved with the cold, standing there and nothing to get, they would starve, you see, only he put them out of it. A wee brown spot back and forth on the white snow.'

Briney crossed himself rapidly after finishing his tea, replaced his cap on his head with a twist of the peak from side to front that settled it firmly in place, pushed his chair back, and rose from the table. 'It's a pity no pup were saved off him,' he said. Then he took his stick and walked through the kitchen door, mindful of some routine obligation calling him away. He had heard about the brown dog before, probably more than once, and was too young and vigorous to sit by the fire listening to accounts of what was past when there was present work to do.

Paddy Rua watched him go out, his own eyes watery and slightly dim as they turned from the darkness of the kitchen to the brighter light coming in through the open door.

'No pup,' he echoed. 'There were no pup saved off him.'

The soft rumble of a tractor, the sound rising as though filtered through the hill air from the valley below, caught his attention for a moment. He turned his face back to the fire, to his recollections of the past, of a time when it was a man's work to walk the rough hills in every weather and see to his sheep, and no machine noise, no whine of car or lorry or rumble of tractor, had ever interrupted the natural sounds of this hill valley, nor marred with their exhaust the soft and everchanging smells of the sloping ground. His mind and thoughts went back to those times easily, and he remembered and spoke of a way of life that was gone, of people and of animals that had died half a century before, or longer, and of beliefs that had lapsed. Life had been different then, lived differently, seen differently. Across the hills there had wandered a race of tall, vigorous men who had shared with their half-wild sheep and cattle more than just a habitat, had shared as well a way of being, had shared some of the wildness, even to the wildness of the strange beasts that were unknown only a few miles further west in the tame and disciplined valleys of the dairy farmers: the water-horses, the winged eels, the sword-nosed water-dogs. He had known many things that were hardly and only reluctantly talked of to anyone from beyond the fringe of the hills.

'Everything's away entirely forebyes what it used to be,' he commented on his own recollections.

At last his thoughts went back to the brown dog, Brock. The dog had been brought, a pup of a few weeks, over the hills from the glen beyond. He had arrived one night at the farm kitchen in the tweed pocket of a hill farmer's jacket, carried over the hill on the chance that he might be wanted somewhere. Placed on the kitchen flagstones he was looked at carefully and curiously for a few moments, he himself looking back quietly at faces never seen by him before.

'A nice wee pup,' was the first comment from one of the group around the hearth.

'Aye,' came the reply. 'He has a wise look about him.'

So, on the ground of his wise look, the 'wee brown pup' stayed, and was known as just that, 'the wee brown pup', until someone noticed that the sheep never shied from him when he came near them, but always turned away from him slowly, scarcely even interrupting their grazing. 'It's because he's like the badger,' an old man – a man old when Paddy Rua was young – had pointed out, 'for the sheep'll not scare before the badger neither.' From that Brock got his name, and had quickly taken to following at Paddy Rua's feet – the brown dog with the red-haired man, as the neighbouring farmers remarked amused at the sight of the small pup following in untaught obedience the tall, thin shepherd. 'The dog's hair brown like the badger,' one of them said, 'and the man's red like the fox.'

Paddy Rua made no effort to train the young dog, but when sheep were being moved or brought together his hands and body spontaneously gestured and spoke in the visual language of the working of sheep. The dog learned without being taught, until one day he moved in a long arc away from Paddy Rua's foot, slowly and quietly out beyond the sheep, rounding them up and taking them away from men and dogs and under his own control.

'He went off then,' Paddy Rua remembered, 'and he took them sheep with him. We were watching to see what would he do, and where would he go. It was the back of

Ben Bwee, and the dog went away from me and left me on the back of the hill, and I did not see him more until I come down to the house here. And him sitting there, and had the sheep put in the yard and all, and him sitting in the gap, keeping them in. He put them in the yard his self, and kept them there. I knew then I had a good dog.'

Paddy Rua soon found that he was right. The dog was a good one, and loyal to the man. Refusing to work for anyone else, he would never leave Paddy's heels. In the worst of storms he stayed with him until all the sheep were seen, or brought together, and when winter blizzard winds blew the snow into deep drifts in the hollows of the northern slopes the dog still remained loyally with the man, leaping and almost swimming his way across or through the drifts, his fur powdered with snow, drops of half-frozen water gathering about his face and nose, blinking into the driving wind, but always staying as long as there was work with the sheep. But most impressive of all was to see the small brown form of the dog climb the snow-covered hill-side that led to the Black Spink, slowly ascend and cross over and above the spink to return, slowly, to the difficult narrow ledges beyond and then, entering one of the ledges, to persuade the trapped sheep to turn and make their way slowly out again.

'Thon was a loyal dog,' Mary interjected, as she took the lid from the iron oven that hung above the fire and peered in to see the condition of the roasting bread.

'And a very gentle one,' Paddy added. 'The only one thing would put him wild was the thunder. He could not abide it, and when he found the rattle of the thunder he was away, and you would not see him more that day. And another was the gun. If there would be hunters about, the dog was away with the first rattle of the gun, up in some wee holes in the spink, hiding until they be gone, till he would come out again.'

'But sure plenty dogs be's that way,' Mary interposed.

'Aye,' Paddy answered. 'Some does.'

It was the dog's alarm at thunder and shots that started the trouble. Paddy had a gun himself, a long-barrelled, straight-stocked muzzle-loader, with which he used to shoot rabbits and hares, or, when luck brought him close enough, an occasional fox. Seeing the dog's fear he used the gun less often, and when unrest began about the country and it was known that searching raids were being made even on farms in the hills he took the gun high up the sloping hill-side and left it in a low rock cave at the foot of the Black Spink. A veil of glossy dark ivy leaves hid the opening from sight.

But one day the first tractor came to the hill valley and with it a frightening collection of engine noises, louder, more astonishing, than either thunder or gunshots. It was a new experience for the inhabitants, and Paddy Rua was not very surprised to find his dog gone. Nor did Brock return for three days.

'He's up in one of them wee holes up under the spink,' Paddy remarked to the old people who had expressed their uneasiness about the dog's long absence. 'He'll soon quit that and come down, when he finds the tractor away.'

But the absent days were unlucky ones for both man and dog. A few miles down the valley a pack of stray dogs had attacked sheep in fenced inland fields, savaging several and leaving deadly open wounds in their sides and hind-quarters. The brown dog was seen among them and positively identified.

'That dog would do no harm,' young, fiery-haired Paddy Rua asserted.

The accuser, a tall shepherd like Paddy himself, shook his head. 'You know yourself,' he said, 'it's the best dogs go to kill sheep the quickest.'

It was the fatal defect of the sheep dog. The gathering

instinct that men put to work for themselves was descended from savage tactics of survival, from a time when all dogs lived only by their skill in hunting, gathering and killing. All sheep farmers knew that. It was common in their talk, and Paddy Rua could not deny the argument.

For a while he was silent. He looked about the farm kitchen at the faces of the old people sitting near the fire or at the bare wooden table. But they only turned to face the fire or rose and walked through the open door.

'All right,' Paddy said at last. 'The dog will be put down.'

When Brock came back the following morning Paddy Rua tied one end of a piece of brown grass rope around the dog's neck, from long practice and custom carefully knotting it in such a way that it could not slip or tighten on the animal's throat, and then tied the other end of the rope to a thin poplar that grew opposite the kitchen door. He climbed the hill to where he had left his gun behind the curtain of ivy leaves and brought it down with him to the house. As he approached, Brock, lying at the base of the tree, raised his head to watch in puzzlement. In the house Paddy Rua slowly removed all traces of the heavy grease he had smeared on and in the gun before leaving it under the rocks. Carefully he measured out a quantity of black powder and poured it into the gun's long single barrel, following it with a bit of wadding drawn from the shoulder of an old and ragged tweed jacket, ramming it firmly into place with a long willow rod. Then he added small grains of shot, and more wadding, and rammed again. The whole process of loading the gun took him almost a quarter of an hour. Satisfied at last, he took the gun and went out.

The dog was gone. A shred of chewed rope was all that remained trailing from the thin poplar.

Paddy Rua stood for a moment without moving, the

long gun balanced in his right hand. Then, without thinking, he raised his eyes to the green slope that rose behind his thatch house, and watched the small brown form of the dog rising slowly upwards, rising and stopping to look back, as he had always done when working sheep, as though this time too he were looking back to the man for gestured instructions, not running impetuously but making his way by slow degrees up the steep hill-side. Paddy Rua stood below and watched the dog ascend until he had reached the spink. Slowly and carefully, as always in the past, the dog rose above the spink, walked along the top, returned down the far side, and walked out on to the narrow ledges, just as he had done so often when turning the trapped sheep out of them. Then he sat.

Paddy Rua started upwards, the loaded gun balanced easily in his hand. He followed the dog's own route, but stopped on the near side of the spink, parallel with the ledge on which the dog sat. Planting his feet firmly into the green sward at the edge of the spink and inclining his tall body slightly forward he raised the gun to his shoulder. For a moment he looked along the barrel until it was steady in his grip, then he fired. The dog collapsed quietly onto the narrow ledge and lay still.

At that moment in his recollections Paddy Rua stopped. A definitive halt in his thoughts intervened. He had no desire to remember or recall any further. A trace of an old man's bitterness and resentment crossed his features. He took off his cap, momentarily revealing the fine white hair that covered his head, and then replaced it firmly with a twist.

'But the other dog were got, you see,' Mary interposed.

Paddy Rua looked into the fire again.

'Aye.'

He paused.

'It weren't many days after that, there were more sheep

tore, and they got the dogs at it. And the brown one in it, it weren't Brock at all. Brock was dead in the spink.'

'It weren't Brock at all,' Mary echoed. 'And then they kilt the ones were doing the killing, but Brock was dead then.'

'Aye, Brock was dead,' Paddy Rua affirmed. He had ended his story, and he pushed himself up, gently, precariously, from his low stool by the hearth, and went to the wooden table in the corner of the kitchen.

But Mary, pouring tea from the old aluminium tea-pot into a plain white cup, went on.

'Weren't it funny, though, about the sheep after that?'

Slowly Paddy Rua began to eat the bread his wife had smeared with butter for him, softening it in his mouth with small sips of the hot tea. For him the story had ended.

But Briney Paddy Rua, returned from the hill, had heard his mother's last words, and resumed again.

'It were funny,' he began. 'But there's Brigid Phil across the river and old Jimmy Wee Jack, the next winter after, when the three yirrols came across the hill, driven ahead of the storm, and went into the spink, they were watching that time, and what was it put the yirrols out again?'

'Ones be saying different things,' Paddy Rua answered. 'You wouldn't know the half of what they be saying.'

A reluctance to remember more had come over him, and the story of the brown badger-like dog was at an end, but Mary, as though echoing her husband's last words, revived the smothered recollections.

'Aye,' she said slowly, pausing in her sweeping of the flagstones, 'ones be seeing different things. You wouldn't know at all what they be seeing.'

Paddy Rua's eyes glowed again with memory, and he raised his hand very slightly above his knee.

'I seen it me self,' he said, 'seen it often after that. And for years more, when the hard winter was in it, there was no sheep lost in the Black Spink, for the wee brown dog were in it still, Brock, to put them out again, a brown spot back and forth on the face of the spink, in snow and all, and the sheep turning and coming out again, quiet, slow, till they be safe.'

His raised hand moved in a small arc, a matter of inches, slowly back and forth above his knee, as though recalling, or trying to recall, the back and forth movement of the brown dog. Mary and Briney watched him and looked, as they seldom did, at his eyes, as though trying to see what he saw. Mary, like many others, had seen the sheep come out of the spink in the midst of heavy winter snow, and even in storms. Sometimes, watching, she thought she saw something moving near them, a small dark form putting them out of the spink. She could never be sure.

Word had slowly gone down the river and into the valley below that the Black Spink had lost its power to trap sheep. Sheep went in, but they came out again. Older men and women nodded quietly over the matter and recalled the history of Paddy Rua's loyal brown dog, wrongly accused, that he himself had shot in the very same spink. Younger men pointed out that rocks had fallen from the spink in a spring thaw and that the ledges had probably widened, allowing the sheep to turn and escape. But in the hills, the hill farmers themselves watched from time to time as sheep came out, and sometimes they followed Paddy Rua's intense look, knowing that he saw something in the spink, something that was working the sheep, turning them around, driving them out. Then they looked back to the spink, saw the sheep moving to safety, and tried to see more. It was not certain that any succeeded.

It was certain, however, that the sheep could not have got out of the spink on their own. Every hill farmer knew that, and some had even seen the sheep move – as sheep never moved – into the driving winds and blowing snow.

'But sure,' Briney said, 'the sheep will always stand with their tails against the storm, never face into it.'

But the story was confused. There were some who said that sheep *were* lost in the spink and that it was only Paddy Rua's old ewes, ones that had been in the spink before and been driven out by the brown dog, and so in a manner trained to come out of it – that it was only those sheep that came out of the spink again. Everyone had a different idea of the truth.

Paddy Rua went back to the fire and sat on his low stool.

'There were no sheep lost in it for years,' he said. 'But then people was talking, saying all kinds of things. Damn, there were no harm in that brown dog that people should take alarm.'

'The priest come up,' Mary explained. 'People were after him to come, I suppose, and he come up to see.'

'Aye,' Paddy Rua resumed. 'The priest come up in his robes and all, a big crowd with him, a *precession*, and up the hill, and beyont, to that lough that's in the hills, and laid him to rest in that lough. That's the wee silvery lough has the trouts in it. Laid him to rest in that lough. That was years ago.'

Paddy Rua stood on his street again looking up towards the Black Spink.

'Right there, where you see that bit of white fleece. That's where a sheep went in last winter and never come out again. That's a bit of the wool. Right next to that, that's where the dog was kilt.' He stopped for a moment, looking towards the spink, and then added his final comment.

'Thon was a loyal dog,' he said.

Later, in the kitchen again, Paddy Rua remembered the gun that had killed the dog.

'Het was the last time ever I used it. I left it then back in the wee cave behind the ivy, and it was only later, after they laid the dog to rest, that I minded the gun, and went up to see about it. And it was there still, but the grease all away off it, and the barrel rusted out. It was rusted out, you see, like fine lace. You would say it was like fine lace. And when I went to lift it out the light went through it like the lace, and it went away then into little bits. Away into tiny bits. Away entirely.'

TOM CROWE

Gaelgeist

You have to put one foot on the ground now and again. Just a touch with the ball of the foot will do, until suddenly a day comes when you can balance and you're free.

The sun glints on the handlebars of the bicycle that has been for so long desired, promised, at last given. The summer is good, blazing over the inherited lakes and the small pedalling boy. In the heat-shimmer the stringbag dragonflies hover and swerve and dog-fight, from rafters and in cool grey ruins the folded bats hang waiting for the night to dawn.

I am Dermot. I am a boy. I am strong. I have a cut on my left knee. My eyes are blue. I have fair hair. I have freckles. I was born eight years ago on the day that Rory O'Connor blew up the Dublin Four Courts. I live in this big house with my father. An old woman looks after me. She is Miss Williams. She is very kind and she isn't afraid of Daddy, but she isn't much fun as she is very old, about fifty, and she can't run very well.

The avenue stretches before him, pale and dusty, a gut connecting the big house with the public road, along which his father is thundering to Ennis in a Model T Ford, hellbent on Miss O'Riordan, the new barmaid at the MacNamara Hotel.

I'm alone most of the time but I'm not always lonely as there is Calnaan who looks after the car. He used to be the coachman. He's the nicest man in the world. My only friends round here are the Tierney girls. They live three miles away. There are five of them. I'm not supposed to

play with them because they're Catholics but we meet and
play at the old castle down by the lake where no one can
see us. I don't see any difference. Grown-ups are stupid
about those things. The way they go on you'd think they
were children. I can take on all the Tierney girls together
in a fight and beat them. I can pull them down in a heap.
They're sissies. There's Arthur Medlicot too. He's very
nice but he lives far away on a mountain and he doesn't
often come here. Visitors, grown-ups I mean, don't come
here much now. When they do I watch and listen. I notice
eveything about them while they talk, every little vein
and pimple, the hairs in their ears and noses. I've forgotten no face that's been here. I remember every voice, all
that's said.

Dermot's family is of the Dal Cais, neither settled nor
planted, but sown by some early tide of migration. Six
hundred years ago they have hurled themselves in a great
rush down a green and rocky hill with Felim O'Connor's
men at Dysert O'Dea and hacked de Clare's force to
pieces in the watery fields below. But the Penal Laws
have enhanced for them the attractions of the Reformed
Church and of the English landlords' daughters. Through
inter-marriage with these, and through judicious purchase
of land, they have taken on the varnish, and finally the
mildew, of Ascendancy. The Gaelic grain cracks the
varnish.

Cahermacrea is a big square house. It looks to the west.
When Dermot stands in the porch there are bright tiles
under his feet. A grey spire rises from the village across
the fields. In the distance, beyond the village, a long high
hill, darkened by trees, stretches across the view like a fat
recumbent sow. Beyond this there is the ocean. Some of
the window-panes of the porch are coloured, others are
plain. He can choose a red world, or a blue or a plain
one. The blue world is heraldic, serenely magical; in the

red world dragons thrash and roar in the ocean beyond the hill. The plain world is the alien truth. It is the way things are.

A few minutes ago, when I was standing with Calnaan in the yard, we watched Daddy driving away. I could see his head through the back window of the car. When Mummy died he wore a black hat for a while, and a black band on his left arm. Now he wears a grey hat on the side of his head and he wears brighter clothes. He thinks I've forgotten.

Dermot does not yet know the boundaries of his father's land. Beyond the big wood there is a lake; beyond the lake there is another wood, and another lake. There are wildernesses of crag and thorn, and paths he has never followed to their end. Through this land the Fergus runs to the Shannon and the sea, a leisurely river, brown, smooth as oil, secret as silk.

Sometimes he takes a little suitcase with him. I don't know where he goes. I'm glad he's gone.

Calnaan has been at Cahermacrea since he was a boy: first a stable hand, then groom, then coachman, now chauffeur. Middle-aged, he is tall and straight and lean, a powerful man. He looks dour, but excitable blood, fierce affections and dislikes, run beneath his skin. He smokes Clarke's Perfect Plug which he flakes into the palm of his hand with a penknife before filling his pipe. He can spit tobacco juice two yards from his mouth. At departures, at funerals and weddings, at all times that touch his heart, tears prickle in his eyes. When this happens his closed lips work furiously; no words come. To fight off the tears, he stamps his feet and waves his arms and shouts at everyone around him. His way of greeting Dermot is to hold out a brown forefinger, tipped with a grimy nail, for the boy to shake. Only once, this very afternoon, had he let his feelings out.

When the car had turned the corner Calnaan took the clay pipe out of his mouth and did a super spit. It went several yards. He said, 'Yerragod, aren't we as well off without him!' His thought just suddenly came out of him before he could stop it and it was funny to hear my own thought spoken by someone else. Calnaan always knows how I feel.

This is the country of Thomond. There is no time inside the moment, as there is no colour inside the rainbow. The swords are still raised in battle in the stony hills at Corcomroe and Dysert O'Dea, but do not fall; the cries are choked with years. The ruin of Cahermacrea Castle, blind and lichenous, stares across the lake, not feeling the picnics or the feet of children. THIS CASTLE WAS BUILT BY TIEGE SECOND SON TO CONNOR THIRD EARLE OF THOMOND AND BY SLANEY O'BRIEN WIFE TO THE SAID TIEGE: ANNO D. Behind it, under the moss, the multitudinous ants are busy with doomed purpose. In the Post Office Miss Casey yawns as she steams open a letter to the big house.

Sometimes Daddy's eyes are funny. There's something you can't make friends with. There's a painted photograph of my great-grandmother on the stairs. Sometimes I stop and look into her face. When I cover the lower part of her face with one hand and her forehead with the other, in the strip between my hands I see Daddy's eyes staring at me and suddenly the old woman starts to come out of the picture and she and Daddy are the same person. When this happens I go and find Calnaan who is always somewhere about and when I talk to him I feel everything is all right. Sometimes, though, even Calnaan isn't enough. When things are really bad I need the other thing. I think of it as a kind of dark toy but it's more like a little black storm, about the size of a football. If I need

it I have to go to it, but once or twice it has almost come
to me.

The avenue runs for an Irish mile through bracken and
primroses, tall trees and bluebells, through the Cragatheen wood, then through a meadow to white iron gates
where the world begins.

We have only candles and lamps at Cahermacrea. It's
dark when I go to bed in winter. I go up the stairs alone
and later Miss Williams comes to say good night. I light a
candle in the pantry and bring it up with me. It's thirty-
seven paces from the pantry to the foot of the back stairs,
forty-nine to the hall stairs. If I go up the hall stairs there
are twenty-nine steps to the first landing, then seventy-
three paces to my bedroom at the end of the landing. I
hold the candle well out in front of me. This is the first
floor. The top floor of the house is empty and I only go
there when I need to, only when it is light, though I go to
a very dark place. From the back door to the foot of the
back stairs it's forty-three paces for me and twenty-five
for Daddy if he's in a good mood. If he's in a bad mood
he does it in twenty-one. There are flagstones on the
passage floor and he has iron tips on his heels. You can
hear them all over the house. I try to be in bed when he
comes back from Ennis but if I've left it too late and I
hear the car coming I run to the back stairs which is a
place he never goes to. He never goes to my bedroom
either. Mummy used to sleep there before she died. I wait
half-way up the back stairs. There's no carpet there and I
get the real smell of the house going back years and years.
Once it nearly came to me there. I was sure I could feel
it. I count Daddy's footsteps from the back door. Twenty-
five if he's in a good mood, twenty-one, long and fast and
heavy, if he's in a bad one. If he meets me before I get to
the back stairs I smile and say, 'Hello, Daddy.' It's always
safer to smile. I never know what he's going to be like.

He's a wizard shot, though, and he can hit a hurley ball right over the house. I'd like to have him on my side if wild beasts were trying to get us. His hands are so strong! I wish I had my full strength now instead of having to wait. If anyone goes for me when I'm grown up I'll fight. I'll fight!

He is approaching the Cragatheen where, even on hot days, there is always a slight chill.

When he's angry his skin doesn't go red, it seems to go dark somehow. Look at that hawk! I know where she lives. I've heard her screaming from her nest in the Cragatheen. She's hovering over the rabbit warren looking for young grazers, her tail stretched to keep herself steady, her wings fluttering. I know that feeling in the tips of my fingers. It must be hard work staying still in the air with your eyes straining down. Will she swoop?

West Clare is made of stone, a ragged shift of grass barely covering her bones. In the Cragatheen the limestone has a skin of moss, tidy as a fitted carpet, treacherous in its welcome. There are narrow deep clefts into which sure-footed animals, sheep and goats, fall and die trapped, staring upwards. With demented thorn there are also tall trees which have taken root somehow, defying rock. It is a mysterious little wood; its strangeness comes on you with a sudden fall in temperature. It is half-way to the front gates.

In winter I have my bath at night before the turf fire in my bedroom. There are rough towels and shiny copper jugs. After I'd been in bed awhile my grandmother, Granny McEnchroe, used to come creeping up to my room. She walked with two sticks and I could hear her coming all the way along the landing because the sticks used to tap the boards at each side of the narrow carpet. I could hear her stays creaking when she came into the room and all she'd say until she'd reached my bed was,

'Sssh!' She'd get hold of my head and put it to her so that my ear was right up against her mouth. Then she'd whisper Catholic prayers so close I could feel her lips moving in my ear. She never said goodnight when she went out, only 'Sssh!' Daddy would have nearly killed her if he'd known, because he and I are Protestants. Granny McEnchroe is dead, and now when I'm in bed Miss Williams sings Protestant hymns into my mouth. Between the two of them I don't know what to make of it. Sometimes before I go to sleep I wish I'd been with the dark toy, just for a little while, but I try not to go to it too often, only at very special bad times. I don't know what it is. I know that it's always there waiting for me. You need someone on your side.

He gets off his bicycle and leaves it lying on its side with the back wheel spinning. He walks quickly into the Cragatheen, glancing neither to right nor left, as if following a line drawn on the ground. Then he stops and looks down into a cleft.

My bedroom is above the kitchen and when I wake up in the morning I can hear Annie Kelly lighting the range. She has a stiff leg and I hear her footsteps, clop-scrape, clop-scrape, clop-scrape. She's the cook. She looks very stern but I can make her shriek by lifting her skirt from behind. I love the rumble of the range because it means that people are about and everything is the same as it was yesterday. When the range is hot you can look down into it through a round hole and see the fire inside it. One morning I got up very early and stole downstairs and peeped into the kitchen at Annie. It was still dark but the glow from the hole was lighting up her face. She didn't know I was there and I felt awful because she looked so sad, staring down into hell.

'Is that what hell is like, Annie?'

'Jesus Mary and Joseph! The Guards! What are you doing, creeping up on me like that!'

'Is that what hell is like?'

'Hell is hotter.'

'What did Jesus do when he went down into hell?'

'Ah, go on with you, Master Dermot, I have the breakfast to cook.'

I think the last time I went to the dark toy was on the day after I'd had the bad dream. I dreamt I had walked into the shrubbery early in the morning and it was the most wonderful morning I had ever known and I knew I'd always be alive and happy for ever. I couldn't look up at the sun, it felt so bright. The grass and all the leaves were shining with little buds of dew and everything was so still I felt I shouldn't move and oh God I didn't want to be separate any more I just wanted to be the same as the grass and the leaves so we'd all be the one thing and nothing could hurt us. And then I saw the Devil. I was so excited I was afraid he'd hear my heart beating. Though I'd never tell it to anyone I'd always felt half sorry for him with nobody on his side, maybe needing a friend. He was quite a long way off, standing very still under my favourite tree, the friendliest tree of all, the laurel that had grown into a kind of house, a safe place with its branches bending over me. His back was turned to me. He wasn't like I thought he'd be at all. He was sort of grey-coloured, like clay. I was afraid to breathe while I watched him. Suddenly he turned round and he was smiling at me, as if he knew I was there all the time. He had such a friendly face! And then I saw that the laurel tree had withered, while all the rest was green, and I was frightened. I ran to the house. Mummy was dead and I knew I'd have to go to Daddy with his strong hands. I ran upstairs and into his bedroom. He was there in bed, but something was wrong. It was Daddy, and it wasn't Daddy. I said, 'Daddy, I've seen the Devil', and I ran to him. Then it was horrible because I saw that he was made of sand. When I got right up to the bed I found that his face and his whole body were crumbling like a heap of sand, just like the sand at the sea.

'You'll have another one with me, Miss O'Riordan.'

'Oh no, thank you, Mr McEnchroe, I couldn't.'

'You will, you will!'

'No, really I cannot. I dare not. I have a light head. I only take a tiny drop sometimes. You had me tipsy last time, Mr McEnchroe.'

'A bird never flew on one wing, Miss O'Riordan, that's one sure fire!'

'Well, that's true for you. All right, so, I'll have something small to keep you company, Mr McEnchroe.'

Miss O'Riordan is creamy, although at twenty-one she has already been well skimmed. She turns her back and pours herself a crème de menthe. She is longing to slosh a good drop of the hard into a tumbler but feels that the liqueur will make a better impression. They are alone in the bar. As she pours the drink she feels the disturbing personality behind her. It is formidable, unrestful, imperious. It seems to fill the air with crackles and sparks. There is too much energy in the room and she would like to open a window to let some of it out. She feels extreme but excited wariness and wonders why her arms are goose-fleshed.

Miss Williams brings me to the Protestant Church in Corofin every Sunday. I hate it, the smell of the prayer books and cushions, the cold grey stone. Miss Williams smells of mothballs in her Sunday clothes. I try to think of God but it's very difficult and I can only think of someone wearing a Garda cap. When I try very hard to think what God looks like I can only see Sergeant Considine of Corofin. Surely he can't look like that?

Sergeant Considine's nose is as red as a beetroot. All the same there's a thought somewhere in my head and I feel if I could get it out I could understand everything. I wish I could think with the whole of my mind. But I don't want to understand everything. I don't really want to understand the dark toy. Not properly, in case it isn't what I think it is. And I'd rather not see it. I'd rather just feel it. No one will ever find out where it is.

A familiar face, a wide brilliant smile, greets him from the bottom of the cleft in the Cragatheen. The goat's skeleton has been there for as long as he can remember. One day, perhaps when pursued, or with the come-hither scent in its nostrils, it had hop-scotched itself into this neat natural grave. Dermot has many times imagined the day. He has watched the last running and skipping over the crags until the trusted foot makes the only slip of a lifetime. He has felt the cramp and the cold spreading through the wedged body, and the hunger, until the eyes glaze and surrender. Even now, he thinks, the bones are trying to run. He peers down at them without compassion. This exercise, many times repeated, is detached. He is not interested in death, but in dead things. He desires detail. He says aloud, 'You're dead and I'm alive.' A bird sings. When Dermot looks up his eye catches the shine of a birch tree. He runs whistling back to his bicycle. He feels exulation, perhaps because death is the stiffener that makes a good strong drink of life.

'All right, so,' she says, raising her little glass. He raises his.

'Let us be lively even if we only live a minute, Miss O'Riordan!'

'Well, that's a good thing to drink to all right.'

'I'd say you're from Cork?'

'I am so. My people are in business there, you know.

My father has a good position. I'm only doing this job for
a cod.'

'I'd rather face wild horses in the street than handle a
Corkwoman.'

A trill of reproachful laughter from Miss O'Riordan.

She rests her elbows on the counter. 'My relief should
be here soon.'

'You live in the hotel, I suppose?'

'Oh I do.'

'It's a good hotel so long as you have the right room. I
hope they've given you a good room.'

'Oh a very nice room, really. Yes.'

I'm glad he's gone. I'm free. I'm riding to the white
gates. This is the first time I'll have been on the public
road by myself. I've always had to have Calnaan with me,
or Miss Williams trotting and fretting and fussing behind
me. Nobody knows where I am this minute. I'll have gone
and come back before they even miss me. I'll leave the
bike in the yard and just walk in, all innocent. If I meet
Daddy coming home it'll be the finish. I'll never see the
bike again. But he won't be back this evening, surely?
Not this evening. Nor tomorrow evening. There's no one
for him to talk to here, only me. The only trouble right
now is Mrs Doyle at the gate lodge, but she sleeps in the
afternoon. She's nearly dead anyway. I'll just open the
gates and ride out without looking to see if she's there.
I'll turn right at the bottom of the village. Then I'll turn
right again at the next crossroads by Clancy's house. Then
I'll be on the road I don't know, from where you can just
see the Burren Mountains heaped in the sky, the road
that goes to where I've never been.

What do these Protestant gentlemen widowers do for
it? If they did it with the maids the talk would be sure to
get out some day. Off to Dublin or London, maybe. Or
do they manage without it? Not this one, surely? An

attractive man all right! He could talk me into anything. If it doesn't happen today it'll be tomorrow. Soon anyway. He'll take me shopping in Limerick. I'll get that outfit I saw in Roche's if it isn't gone. Maybe he'll take me to Dublin? London, even? If it isn't today it'll be tomorrow, or the next day. Or next week. Such an attractive man! But my God, the eyes! What sort of a beast is it inside him? Anyway it'll be soon. It'll be very soon. His sort can't wait. They're hell-raisers, real hell-raisers.

Dermot opens the white gates, mounts his bicycle for the first time alone on the forbidden public road and pedals towards the village. He has defied a huge imperative and taken his first real risk. He rides down the village street. An old woman straightens her back to gaze at him, a hand shading her eyes. Johnsie Frawley, the blacksmith, just back from Ennis, gives a tipsy roar. From others there are cries of astonished greeting. 'Master Dermot! Well, well!' He may survive privilege and the hail of blessings that it brings, but his pores are still open to flattery. He knows nothing of poverty, of how it makes you smile when there is no smile. He meets friendliness head on, thirsting, basking in the illusion of order. He reaches the end of the village and turns right. Now he is on the strange road that leads to a wilderness of rock. Cahermacrea land is still on his right but soon he will have passed its boundary. Along the skyline the hazy Burrens sleep.

When he turns a corner he sees a jaunting-car and quickens his pace to get a closer look. It carries two men, one of them lolling, his head moving loosely with the swaying of the car, the other upright and stiff, holding the reins. Both wear tattered hats with the brims turned down. These men have a quality of strangerhood. There is something in them that takes the trust out of Dermot. Even from behind them he can sense something quite

different from the village people. A message that they are
alien from him seems to come from their backs. 'Take
care,' it says, 'we are not for each other, we will never
mix.' The driver's back is very thick with rolls of fat as if
he is wearing tyres round his body. The hairs on his
creased nape are dark. Dermot decides to overtake. He
pedals his blue bicycle a little faster until he is close
behind and his nostrils catch the smell of the horse. He
hesitates, then makes a spurt. He draws level with the off-
side wheel of the car and feels that he is doing an awful
thing: he is where he should not be, alone on his bicycle
on the public road and the road seems to belong to the
man holding the reins. He pedals faster until he can see
the driver's face. The man flicks the trotting horse with a
whip held lightly in his right hand. He is swarthy and
heavy-jowled, staring into the distance. Dermot gets a
glance from the corner of a swivelled dark eye. Then the
head turns and the face takes a full but expressionless
look at the boy. Dermot smiles. There is no response,
neither smile nor frown. When he makes the final effort
to overtake Dermot is humiliated by seeing the lash of the
whip glide across his left wrist. It is little more than a
venomous caress, as if a snake has licked him and he
hardly feels it, but the deft lazy action carries a command.
He looks up at the man, hoping for a laugh or a wink to
redeem the moment; but the heavy jowls do not move
and the face looks straight ahead. Dermot freewheels and
drops back. He stops and gets off his bicycle to watch the
jaunting-car and the two men driving towards fields of
rock, into old battlegrounds and places of hearsay.

Although the sun is high in the full strength of summer
there is an eeriness and the men seem to melt into the
light. A little flurry of air hovers around Dermot's head
for a few moments with its familiar, unspeakable smell.

He crooks his arms as if to hold it to him to get comfort, but it has gone.

At this moment, in a bedroom in the MacNamara Hotel, Dermot's father shoots forth his seed, nourishing complexity with this Protestant irrigation of a Catholic womb. There are brass knobs on the bedstead. In one of these orbs he catches a glimpse of his contorted features. Shrill voices come through the window overlooking the square of the Pro-Cathedral, voices of children in the bare-footed thirties, playing in the dust.

With his head down Dermot rides back through the village. He passes through the white gates again. From her small window Mrs Doyle watches him, motionless, a silent old woman with nearly a lifetime of unexpressed bewildered envy behind her. Dermot rides fast through the Cragatheen. In the haggard at Cahermacrea he finds – oh, thank goodness! – safe Calnaan, the always, always Calnaan.

'. . . rough bad men, Calnaan, really rough. The driver had a terrible face. You felt there was murder right down in his soul.'

'Oh Jay!'

'He never smiled. His arms were as thick as your thighs.'

'Were they, faith?'

'If you'd been there and he'd gone for me, what'd you have done, Calnaan?'

'I'd have hit him a blow in the lug of the ear.'

'Would it have knocked him out? Would he have been knocked out?'

'What knocked out! He'd have been knocked into the middle of next week.'

'We'd have beaten them both?'

'Me and you could beat the world.'

'Show me your muscle, Calnaan.'

Calnaan rolls up his right sleeve, stretches out his arm and slowly brings his clenched fist to his shoulder. Under the white skin a knotty ball gathers and swells to the size of a turnip.

'Calnaan!'

There is silence between them. Again there is a little flurry of air. Dermot's thought is drawn away.

'Look at me a minute.'

Dermot looks and finds Calnaan's eyes searching his face. He has never seen Calnaan's eyes like this, narrowed to slits.

'Sometimes I wonder whether you're growin' up or growin' down.'

'How do you mean, Calnaan?'

'There are times it's like you'd lost a bit of your*self*. D'you know?'

'I *think* I know, Calnaan.'

'D'you ever go messin' about in some bad old place?'

'Why?'

'Times I get a smell out of you. I don't mind a bit of honest old dirt, but this smell, it's not natural.'

'All smells are natural, and I have a bath every night. Ask Miss Williams.'

'This is a rotten old house.'

'It's a *lovely* house!'

Friendship is dying.

'Same thing happened to your father.'

'What?'

'He changed, like. When he was a boy like yourself. There's be times he'd go some place in the house and no one could find him at all. Ye're a mixed bunch. Ye were Gaels once, true Irish. Since ye turned ye've never had luck. Hare and hounds don't mix. It's like something's tryin' to get at ye, drawin' ye back. There's something

wrong in Cahermacrea, I'd like to scour the house like a
dirty pan.'

'Changed?'

'Ah, he's not the son his mother bore. It's like he
changed into . . . into some class of a . . .'

Calnaan scratches his head.

'A devil? Calnaan, I had a dream . . .'

Calnaan puts his hand on the back of Dermot's head.

'Mind yourself, asthore.'

Suddenly, with such force that it is painful, he pulls the
boy's head hard against his ribs.

'God blessoo!'

It is four o'clock. Lakes and ruins are asleep. Every
leaf is still. The hawk swoops, the baby rabbit feels the
talons and the meticulous thrust of the beak. He screams
and is borne away.

> 'Now the day is over,
> Night is drawing nigh,
> Shadows of the evening
> Steal across the sky.'

Miss Williams's hands form a funnel between Dermot's
cheeks and her own. Her lips are very close to his. She
sings out of tune and her breath is a little sour, though all
her life she has drunk the sweet milk of faith. Dermot
cannot forget the lick of the whip. It will be there for
ever. It is not the touch of the whip that has disturbed
him, but the languorous authority behind its application.
The incident has pulled askew the whole cat's-cradle of
the day's happiness.

> 'Now the darkness gathers,
> Stars begin to peep,
> Birds and beasts and flowers
> Soon will be asleep . . .'

I'll wait a few minutes after she's gone, and then I'll get up. I'll go to the dark toy. I'll tell you one thing for certain – no matter what happens, no matter what you've done, *you need someone who's always on your side.*

> 'Grant to little children
> Visions bright of Thee.
> Guard the sailors tossing
> On the deep blue sea . . .'

For goodness sake get on with it!

> 'Comfort every sufferer
> Watching late in pain;
> Those who plan some evil
> From their sins restrain . . .'

Miss Williams tucks in the sheet and quietly leaves the room. Her footsteps grow faint along the landing. One minute more and she will be down in the drawing-room. It is time to go to the dark toy. Dermot gets out of bed, very slowly opens the door and softly shuts it behind him. He steals bare-footed to the stairs that lead to the top of the house. As he rises, step by careful step, the furniture and decoration grow sparser, like vegetation on a mountain. There are no pictures on the walls of the first flight, no wallpaper on the second. On the third the carpet withers. The sap of the house is falling. He reaches the bare boards of the top landing. There is a faint smell of absence.

One day when Medlicott was here he said it was the smell of Dead Maid.

Dead Maids. Captives. Twelve shillings a month, their keep and clothing; black dress, black stockings, cap and apron. Captives, dying in captivity.

Dermot creeps to the front of the house and into a

room where the floor is littered with the junk of dead generations: boxes and trunks in which once-cherished things have grown tired and trivial. Old toys, a phonograph and other mechanical engines full of forgotten purpose, made with the care of years ago, heavy, with many shining parts, seem on the verge of marvellous precise function, but have withdrawn all co-operation. Through the window Dermot gazes at the spire across the fields. The heart has gone out of the day. He leans his head against the wall. These walls are nearly three feet thick. Surely, surely they will stand for ever?

Yes, I am alone, but not lonely. Even if Calnaan wasn't here I could stop loneliness. I can make things up. I can make up people. I can make them talk. I can gather crowds of them around me. I can make up worlds. I can make things happen.

He tip-toes to the back of the house, to the maids' deserted quarters. He enters a small room and stands still, excitement rising. He goes to a corner of the room. With his finger-nails he prises open a wooden door which is flush with the wall and crawls into a small cupboard, closing the door tightly behind him. Total darkness. In the side of the cupboard there is an inner recess, its opening little more than a hole, not big enough even for a child to enter. Here no light has ever been. With tender caution Dermot puts his arm through the hole and for a few moments allows his hand to hang limply in the emptiness. He withdraws it and squats on the floor, waiting patiently. A turbulence begins to grow in the recess. No solid thing is moving, just a frenzy of air. Dermot waits. His whisper is a continuous sibilance. 'You're still there. You're on my side, you're always, always on my side.' Then it rushes to him. Its form is faintly palpable, its shape nothing more than the periphery of its convulsive agitation, yet he is able to contain this congestion of darkness in his arms like a ball of black tempest. It generates a foul, companionable smell, a wind of inescapable kinship which has passed through the charnel house of Irish history. It brings him comfort, for each time he goes to it it draws from him a little of his troublesome, estranged identity. He keens on a thin, high note, swaying and rocking on his haunches. It seems that a crowd is gathering around him. There is the painful beginning of articulation. From a host of voices there come the rough syllables of a language struggling for rebirth. Dermot doesn't understand them, these syllables of his race.

DESMOND HOGAN

The Birth of Laughter

Walking through the garden she carefully chided the trees, pulling bushes from her way, distracting leaves from her hair. That she was back here hardly made sense to her. That she was unafraid was not safe to contemplate. Being here was easy. She looked about. Light stole through her hair. She was twenty-two. An observer would have conceived her as being very beautiful, hair twisted and knotted in gold pigtails.

A butterfly rose. She stared, haunted by the pallor of its wings. She laughed. The child inside her would be a girl, a brown girl like the black babies in Roman Catholic national schools, nodding on boxes which were filled with money for the foreign missions. The butterfly waved, danced, coaxed. She ran. Her hand reached towards it. Light caught her topaz ring. The colours in it sparkled, green, orange, brown. Catherine laughed. She laughed until the entire garden heard her laughter. Her body froze. Was she really laughing? Was this voice really hers? She waited. Nothing happened. No one took her. A blind aftermath of laughter rang through her. She laughed again, raced again until the entire garden welled with imaginary butterflies and her hair spun imaginary roses.

She stopped. She walked. She felt trees again, bushes again, a lazarus reborn to sensation. She walked slowly as though in a trance. It was like slow-motion in a childhood film. Catherine Findlater you are reborn to the exquisite touch of things she told herself. Catherine Findlater you are saved.

The grass by the stream was already gold. Some straws held themselves high like August wheat. She knelt by the water. Her face glowed. She smiled. She smudged her features with her fingers. She smiled again. Laughter was imminent. This time she did not laugh. She screamed. A figure rose behind her. She looked up quickly. It was Adoe. He embraced her. His skin was stretched and light brown over brittle bones. His arm held her to him. His shirt was white. They strolled through the garden. In lighter moments of remembrance she could recall Aunt Madeleine recite lines of balmy love poetry by her friend William Butler Yeats or the Song of Solomon or recourse to Byron. She strolled now with her Indian lover and husband. Laburnum was bursting, magnolias hanging, lilac already sheathing bushes with white.

'You're all right. You're fine,' he said.

Sometimes she'd stare at him and ask him why he'd brought her here. 'You must come back. For your own good.' She was frightened and crying. She'd been left the house by her Aunt Madeleine. True, she'd grown fond of the lilac there. True, she'd placed a big rubber doll among the snowdrops there, left it languishing, sticking pins into it, hoping to draw blood to colour the snowdrops red. In other words she'd been a child here. But Aunt Madeleine's grave was too close for comfort, grey Wexford stone.

In a Dublin flat she'd say, 'No. I can't go back. I can't.' One night when Adoe was out performing in a play – *Ghosts* by Ibsen – she'd risen screaming. The whole ritual had risen in her. She's begun sweating. She'd been a month pregnant. She'd gone to the window. It had been in Fitzwilliam Square. She'd pushed up the frame. Sweat was emerging like a shadow from her skin. She'd wished herself dead upon the pavement below. She'd made to throw herself. He'd caught her. He'd forced her on the bed. He'd made love to her. Her mind had given way. She'd dreamt of mice, many mice in the castle long ago. Mice were crawling at her feet. Mice were running beneath and betwixt her. She'd woken as though to scream. He'd been beside her. She'd smitten his nipple with her right forefinger. It had been a butterfly. It had come alive to her. She'd kissed it. She'd slept upon his stomach.

A real butterfly waved by now. 'Look,' she cried delightedly. 'Isn't it pretty.'

'She,' Adoe corrected her, 'It's a she. A she butterfly.'

'How do you know?'

'Isn't it obvious?'

Whereas the previous butterfly had been merely white this one was many-coloured. 'Lovely,' Catherine cried, 'Lovely. Lovely. Lovely.' She turned to Adoe. His lips burgeoned with a red like summer raspberries. She kissed him. He held her. Her laughter became tears now; tears shook from her. Again the fear rose in her. She stared into the density of Adoe's chocolate-brown eyes.

'Do not forsake me.'

'No,' his voice was a whisper.

The french windows behind her held a shadow of lace. Catherine began sobbing and as she did the french windows splintered with red, red from a drawing-room geranium. 'Adoe,' she clutched him. The child started coming. She held him. She collapsed.

Avenues of cypresses in the summer sun; these were her first memories. These cypresses darkened; they held back – like a deluge. Her mother would take her hand, dolled up in a grey shirt and white blouse and persuade her through these shadows. Catherine would look – scared. Her mother had been a parson's daughter from Offaly, singularly quiet and inoffensive. She'd married George

Findlater after meeting him at a midsummer's party in Tipperary, south of Offaly, north of Wexford. The party had occurred beside a lake. The hills had been lit by fires, burning for Saint John's Eve, bronzed young men, disgorging themselves of shirts, jumping over the flames and shadows of flame and evening fire imminent on the lake. The man she'd met had been attractive, rather like one would imagine Emily Brontë's father to have been attractive. He'd been distant and contemplative of the sunset; they'd courted. He'd driven from Wexford in a Ford coupé which resembled a ramshackle funeral car. They'd married when apples had been burnished in the County Wexford glades of George's home. They'd honeymooned in Galway; on a lake beside a convent school where nuns wandered about reading brevaries, draped like blue whales. They'd made love. They'd conceived Catherine there. They'd returned to Wexford.

'There has been much suffering in the Findlater family,' her mother had always said to Catherine. If one looked one could see the off-set of such suffering on her mother's face. She'd arrived in Wexford to live in a lowly decaying castle. Portraits had exploded about her like decaying cartoons. Suits of armour had astonished her with their glamour of light. More than anything she'd been awed by the garden, by the richness of shade there, by the effervescence of grass. She'd stare as Madeleine held her parties.

To these parties would be drawn the élite of Ireland and Britain, young men with faint gladness, neckties and cravats bursting. These young men came from the hills, from the Midlands, from castles and fortresses, the last of the Anglo-Irish peers. They'd come with wolfhounds, with gangling strides, with fat and expensive cigars whose odours suggested Berlin and Paris. Madeleine would

entertain them with the full force of the servant popula-
tion of the house. She'd lay tables with cakes of strawberries and cream, escalating cakes, bilberry wines; lavender
and roses decorating the sheer white and the sheer length
of the table. One could hear her voice crackle. 'The horn
of plenty,' she'd cry and Catherine's mother, daily becoming more and more aware of local resentment, realized
that the Findlaters' access to wealth was based on Famine,
on centuries-old greed. Once a Findlater had wandered
to Ireland in dainty pantaloons with Edmund Spenser,
recognized this valley with its rolling glades and gossamer-
like hawthorn as being a place of serenity, set up home
here, ransacked the district, drew much wealth to the
house. The Findlaters had lost their title through a row
with Queen Victoria and some of them had taken to the
Church, a black whispering Protestantism. During the
famine the family was beset by wraith-like peasants har-
anguing the door like famished wolfhounds. They
received potatoes, soup. Their eyes haunted the occu-
pants of the house like the dots on a peacock's feather.
'Remember 1798,' the eyes seemed to say. 'Remember
the young man who rode into your garden and died
among the apple-blossoms, wounded in Wexford by the
redcoats.' Maids would firmly replace the leaden locks,
shutting out the offending evenings of famine Ireland.

'The horn of plenty!' Madeleine's voice reverberated
through the garden even after she'd taken up her bags
and flown to Paris in an aeroplane from Shannon airport.
'The horn of plenty!' Catherine's mother had been
haunted by Madeleine's silken clothes as she'd wandered
about the castle. In the same year her husband had died
of a heart attack, she herself had begun to grow weaker
and George's two sisters, living in two separate houses in
the village, had taken to flights of madness, wandering in

the night, both in nightgowns, speaking of ghosts, of wolf-hounds, of legendary Irish heroes. Both had been diverted to a mental hospital in Enniscorthy where they ate fresh tomatoes and stared, blissfully, and hauntedly, at the river below. George's third sister Madeleine, likewise owning a small house in the village, had disappeared to Paris so, as Catherine grew up, holding her mother's hand as she strolled down avenues of cypress trees, all she'd known of Aunt Madeleine was an awesome photograph in the living room, Madeleine's hair long and black and flowing and her lips, smiling even in middle-age, flushed and shot through as though by blood.

These were her earliest memories, sitting in the living room in winter or summer, her mother reading her huge handsome volumes of Hans Christian Andersen or the Grimm brothers. If it were summer the windows would be open and bees singing across the patterns of the carpet. If it were winter huge fires would be rumbling and Catherine's mother would occasionally lean towards the blaze and pick chestnuts from the turf. Then her mother died. Catherine had been five. She died almost as gently and as devotedly as ogres came and went in fairy-stories or as young women with long golden hair had been carried off to round towers where they waited for handsome princes to free them.

The cause of death – later established – was a lung complaint. Catherine watched her burial. It had been winter. She clutched a doll and shed some tears and watched water springing like seeds from branches. It had been raining. Servants were there in force. Wexford spread. 'If one looked far enough,' Catherine had thought, 'one could see strawberries.'

As a rule strawberries did not arrive in Wexford until June. That year had been no exception. Catherine had waited for strawberries, their seedling red, and knew also that her Aunt Madeleine, previously unidentified, was arriving to look after her. All she'd known of Aunt Madeleine was her books, her photograph. It was known Aunt Madeleine was the author of books. They lingered in the house – like ghosts.

She arrived one afternoon, drawing up in a hearse-like taxi. Her face had seemed blotched and bewildered. Catherine had stared, teddy-bear loose in her fingers. Madeleine had beheld her. Her eyes had a lucidity and yet a horror which burnt into memory.

Madeleine Findlater, authoress, author of historical romances, a study of the tarot and a biography of an obscure Rumanian poet who died in 1937.

Catherine's eyes opened – she was in a hospital. Nurses studied her. There was one who held a glass of water. She recognized Adoe behind a black doctor. She reached for him. She collapsed.

Five years old she'd been then and innocent of her aunt's past. The castle was sold to an American millionaire who brought a blue-haired mistress to convalesce there from an attack of multiple sclerosis and who then abandoned it, allowing snowdrops in spring to overshadow its lawns, a lonely cold twirling battalion of incestuous males. Such was the fate of the Findlater castle, a sort of companion to Catherine's growing years. She'd come and look at it, tracing herself a path from the national school, feeding herself on Nestlé's chocolate, finding her hands growing sticky, rubbing them in daisies.

At school Miss Rafter would recite the poetry of Yeats. 'Though I am old with wandering through hollow lands and hilly lands I will find out where she has gone.' Miss Rafter had pretty blonde hair, a lock of which fell from her forehead. She'd wear blouses as fine as buttercups and her eyes always seemed shaking and about to flow with tears. Children stared at her, the few Protestant children of the locality. One day she left and years later Catherine saw her again, tempered by age but still lovely.

On going home Catherine would also hear about Yeats. Aunt Madeleine spoke freely on the subject. He used to visit the castle. He would dine there and speak about The Golden Dawn. In the 1930s, in Aunt Madeleine's youth, he would occasionally visit, push white hair from his forehead and recall his own youth and early temptresses as apple-blossom dipped from a bough. Aunt Madeleine would produce photographs in evidence of Yeats' visits. They hadn't been altogether clear but the white laid table on the lawn was in evidence, a shower of strawberries, and a poet, leaning on a cane, staring into an unbeckoning afternoon.

Sometimes visitors would come, they also speaking of Yeats. A priest from a strange religion arrived in a long black dress and with a flowing beard. 'Russian Orthodox' was the name of the creed and Aunt Madeleine had expounded with him on the craft of Yeats. One or two visitors arrived from England. They spoke of the Queen. Aunt Madeleine had prepared a jelly dessert and they'd partaken of it, speaking of the Queen's imminent visit to New Zealand. That evening in bed Catherine had recourse to nightmare. She kept seeing her mother; her mother was running through the woods. Her mother was weeping. 'Mother.' She'd woken. She'd aired a slight tremor. She'd run down the stairs. She'd opened the kitchen door. She'd opened the drawing-room door. Inside was dark. Inside Aunt Madeleine was seated by the table, hands outstretched on the table, those of her visitors linking with hers and a candle lit and a glass on the table, moving.

* * *

Her eyes opened once more.

She could hear a nurse saying. 'It will be a while yet.'

Her body slipped. Sleep now was kind; it flowed within her – like a river.

She understood no pain; all that was happening was happening from a force of persuasion. She had worked so hard for this moment, this moment when the past could be reckoned with and the present – for she knew it now – was the birth of a baby.

'Susan.' Madeleine had addressed her mother. She could still hear the voice of Madeleine cutting through the dark. 'Are you unhappy?' Catherine had conceived of that moment many times, a horrible crash, a scream, her scream. Madeleine had taken her and put her to bed. Sweat had oozed.

'Be easy child,' Madeleine had said. 'Be easy.'

At the door the eyes of the English couple had stared, a point of fixation. They'd seemed so inane that Catherine had quietened, reflecting on the human race. She was ten now. She was growing up.

She'd run in the fields, she'd talk to sheep, she'd sit in the garden eating honey. She'd dance to the music of the gramophone as Aunt Madeleine typed an essay about Bucharest for some English newspaper.

Visitors were scarce now; Aunt Madeleine was drinking port and murmuring to herself and one summer's day in the garden she'd begun weeping as bees hummed about her. That had been one of the first of these flights. Many followed. Her lips were growing redder from port and her voice more crackly. A woman who'd been no more than a guardian for Catherine was emerging as a personality. The shock of seeing Madeleine talk to her mother had given way to curiosity. Catherine would stand at the top of the stairs as Aunt Madeleine recited poetry in a blue nightdress at the bottom of the stairs. It was not poetry by Yeats but poetry by an obscure Rumanian poet about whom Aunt Madeleine had written a book. Sometimes she'd cackle away in words of Rumanian, mixing them with remarks about wine, about bridges in Paris, about church railings in Trieste. Aunt Madeleine was becoming obsessed.

One day at the gramophone was playing 'Tales from the Vienna Woods' Catherine had found Aunt Madeleine sleeping in a chair in the garden, port slipping from her mouth like blood.

The following winter Catherine had trailed to school. Aunt Madeleine was spending much of her time in bed. Catherine would make her cocoa and Aunt Madeleine would speak about the jackdaws outside. 'Such noisy creatures,' she'd remark, 'such noisy creatures.'

Catherine was now in the position of looking after Aunt Madeleine. Sometimes when Catherine entered her room she looked more like a man. One day Aunt Madeleine had risen from her bed, put on her good clothes, brought Catherine to Dublin. They'd climbed Nelson's pillar, they'd munched a strawberry ice-cream in a café beside the bridge. They'd walked down avenues sprouting with blossom. Both of them had sometimes stared, bewildered at the beauty of the city. Catherine was now twelve. Having seen enough films at the cinema in Carrick-on-Suir to have acquainted her with devious pasts she was now beginning to realize Aunt Madeleine had a divided history. That day on an avenue near Trinity College an old man with a white beard had called Madeleine. He'd come running towards her. He'd had gold in his white hair and a cap on his head. Madeleine had stared at him. Her eyes had been like frightened butterflies. 'Peter,' he'd kept saying. 'Peter.' Aunt Madeleine had kept babbling.

She'd spoken of books, of a novel she had begun writing. Eventually she'd said, 'I killed him. I know that.'

The train back to Wexford had taken them through countryside burning with spring. Aunt Madeleine had kept muttering under her breath, 'When all the wild summers were in her gaze.'

As summer approached she worked continuously on her novel, seated by a table in the garden, a silk robe with an orange sun on the back flowing on her, her narrow fingers tapping the typewriter. One day her manuscript had flown away and she'd shrieked, pursuing the sheaves until she had the last one, sodden in a pond where a water-lily was about to jump open.

A publisher had arrived from London, a newspaper man. There were photographs of Aunt Madeleine sitting on park benches in Trieste in the English Sunday papers. She had been rediscovered. Her years peeled away in the garden. There was a pink robe she wore that summer and tulips sprung like strangers. Catherine was now growing up in a world of the literary élite.

Madeleine's novel was a huge success. Others of her books were reprinted and one day in autumn some years later Catherine and Aunt Madeleine had packed their bags and left for London. Aunt Madeleine had been awarded a literary prize. Catherine had been grabbed from boarding school and with Aunt Madeleine she'd crossed the Irish Sea. They'd landed in Wales, taken a train to London and there stayed in a house white as wedding cake in a square where leaves were falling and Catherine bemoaned the fact she could not appear in *The White Horse Inn* at school.

She hadn't been away in boarding school long enough not to notice that behind the beautiful features which were reforming on Aunt Madeleine's face was fear.

Sometimes on visits to the school those features had seemed blotched and awkward.

What was it Aunt Madeleine was seeking to hide? Where were the secrets? Catherine would have wandered the house demanding answers had she not had a fleeting fancy for a teacher at school who looked like Marianne Faithful.

To the house in the square had come men grown old before their time and women young in years but old in expression. London's literary world had convened. Catherine had attended the odd lesson given by a Rumanian in Bedford Square and returned to find pictures of Yeats on the wall and old men speaking of magic.

She had stopped outside the oak doorway to the living room one day. 'Peter was a man of remarkable charm,' an old man was saying. 'He was one of the most remarkable poets of his time. Some day that shall be known.'

That evening Aunt Madeleine had stalked about; young men were coming to the house now. They were driving up in red sports-cars and Aunt Madeleine was wearing mini-skirts. She'd had power over age. She was as one of the young models of London. She had been seeing a particular young man with hair like summer sunsets, gold and pale and partly blond. He'd been angelic. He'd worn red handkerchiefs in his pockets and occasionally a young woman telephoned, inquiring for him. Aunt Madeleine had taken him to her bedroom more than once. Once they'd screamed at each other. He'd left. Aunt Madeleine had stood on top of the stairs weeping. Catherine had touched her. 'We're going,' she'd said. 'We're going looking for him.'

In the following days Aunt Madeleine had swept along to Greek Orthodox churches, to Russian Orthodox churches. She'd lit candles before icons. She'd whispered devotions. She'd summoned five older people to the house and performed a séance. This time Catherine had sat in the room next door reading a book by Hans Christian Andersen, realizing for the first time her aunt's all-out preoccupation with the dead. There'd been the séance with her mother when she'd been ten. There'd been the pictures of Isis among the teddy-bears of childhood, there'd been chants her aunt had uttered, there'd been herbs she'd chosen on hills in Midsummer. All this had been submerged in the stronger occultism of the area, crumbling castles, decaying teachers, whispering flowers.

Aunt Madeleine was now making no secret of it. Catherine had listened that evening. 'It's no good,' her aunt had said next door. Catherine had wandered through the house and picked up her aunt's book on the tarot, opened it on the hanged man, an illustration of a noose about a young man's neck. 'The force of tribulation is in this card,' the commentary had read. Catherine had thumbed further through the book.

Outside a wind was blowing up and she'd realized, page after page, that herein was contained a history. She'd been fifteen. She'd gone to the window, longed for Ireland, knew her life was beginning.

That evening Aunt Madeleine had announced, 'We're going to Europe.'

'Why?' Catherine had demanded.

'To seek him out.'

'He' was Peter. 'He' no longer was young men who called to the house or dapper princes with red limousines in London who took Aunt Madeleine out. 'He' was Aunt Madeleine's past.

Afterwards she would say to Adoe, what you grow up with you accept.

She'd accepted Aunt Madeleine, she'd lost herself in books, in primroses, in countryside. Now was the time, a sprightly fifteen-year-old she'd demanded questions, she'd asked herself the reason for Aunt Madeleine's extraordinary conglomeration of behaviour.

In later years she would meet young men in Dublin living rooms who would quote Henry James to her. Certain quotations made sense. Quotations which indicated that there is a moment when personal search commences, search of roots, search of environment, search of past, present and sense of self.

She'd studied the reflection of her hair in a dark taxi which drove through London that evening, blonde on black, autumn outside, a penetrating chill in the leaves, in the faintness of light under a moonless sky.

They'd crossed to Ostend.

'Where are we going?' Catherine had asked. Her aunt had looked at her. She'd been wearing white. Her eyebrows had been defined in black. She'd looked at Catherine and, as she had, Catherine had been astounded by the rocking of the ship.

'We're seeking him out. Haven't I told you?'

'Him.' Peter. That moment Catherine had assimilated all. There'd been a man. He'd ruined Madeleine's life. He'd haunted her.

They'd arrived in Brussels. It had been late at night. A shop had been open and they'd indulged in chips with mayonnaise on top. A woman with a kindly face had served them.

'I was in love,' Aunt Madeleine had said, 'I was in love. It was after my first book appeared. I was walking down Southampton Row one day with a rose on my dress when I saw him. I'd seen him in the newspaper the previous Sunday. I said, "Hello." Peter was one of those people who emerge from nowhere. In the twenties there were many. G. I. Gurdjieff was one, men without backgrounds. Peter claimed to be Rumanian. I wrote about him as such. But he wrote in English. He had one of those faces that had registered wine, women, earthquakes, revolutions. He fell in love with me and I fell in love with him. We wrote to each other. We exchanged notes under chandeliers at crowded dinner parties. We confronted something in one another. What would you call it? That not easily defined substance, a soul. In Peter I saw the fruition of my youth, my work, my ability to write. He likewise saw such things in me. His work gravitated towards the very fine; there were whispers in his poetry of all kinds of occultism. From my background I was acquainted with the herbs of Wexford, the cards of the tarot, the cult of Isis. I'd spoken to Yeats of séances he'd observed in his youth and despite his warning I took part in the rites – at first but mildly then acquainting myself with the souls of the lonely, those who always come at will to the room wherein a séance is taking place. These were the things of my youth, certain potions for certain ailments, and a deck of cards that read the past as well as the future. But Peter's connections were more intimate with the supernatural. He'd discussed evocation of evil with dignitaries of a certain cult known to touch on a world of which many people were aware at the time, a world wherein were amassing forces of evil which were going to take over the world. These people wished to control these forces. Perhaps out of good, perhaps because of interest in power. Talk of power was everywhere, power over words, power over people. Peter and I journeyed up and down the east coast of Ireland; we stopped in houses where we took part in séances and spoke to dead elders. We travelled to Europe; 1936. The year Mussolini rode into Abyssinia I rode into the Mediterranean with Peter on a horse at Saintes Maries de la Mer in the South of France. It was in October, in honour of Saint Sarah, patroness of gipsies. We were on a voyage, in the heat of autumn we drank wine, smoked Turkish cigarettes; there were cracked mirrors in every little hotel but in our way we knew we were projecting elegance, that extraordinary quality only young people can project, a perfect image of life, a stability the wise can never know. There were bottles of red wine and young men in white suits. Europe was going to pieces but we travelled like patterns on wallpaper to Cairo; we, a poet and a young lady writer, were part of the effulgence of Europe before collapse. We were the cool flowers before the "bloody rimmed waters" rose. Such knowledge forced us to pray one day; in a church in Sardinia, the two of us on wooden pews.

'Going back on our path however we were drawn into knots of Peter's friends, those with contacts in Scotland, England, Ireland.

'At first our meetings with these people were friendly.

'Then they were otherwise. Taking part in a séance in Gibraltar I knew our mission was not holy; Peter's friends were trying to control the spiritual rather than allowing the spiritual to control them. They were delving into the interior of a spiritual landscape, a landscape born of evil. They were victims of a desire that surpassed sanity. They desired a say in a new ascendancy, an ascendancy of evil.

'How can I tell you why I became involved? I became involved out of love. I loved Peter. He loved me. He was more victim than I. He'd dabbled in something. It had become his life!'

Catherine had folded her nightdress carefully the following morning. She and Aunt Madeleine had let the light in. They'd boarded a train to Paris. It was to be the location. They were going to try to contact Peter.

'Love,' Aunt Madeleine had explained, 'is a strange thing. It occurs less frequently than we imagine. It is the most surprising and most nourishing thing in life. It is indeed holy. That is why I want to go back and contact Peter. I loved him. When we arrived in Paris in the spring of 1937 Peter began thrusting himself into the company of a girl mixed up in his group. This group was making strange wooden instruments. They were preparing for a final evocation of the forces they'd attained to. I recognized waywardness in myself. Though not a Catholic I prayed at Sacré Coeur. I knew he loved me. About me he'd written the finest of his poetry. Now this distortion was coming over him. He was leaving me to drink wine alone in a hotel, going off, making love to a Finnish girl. I forgave him twice. The third time I said I was leaving. It was in the room in the hotel. It was nearly June. There were roses, partly yellow, partly red. He seized them and stuck the thorns on his wrists until the red of his blood commingled with the red of the roses. I took a bag and made to go, stayed with him, made love, knew there couldn't be anything in my life more holy than this. I awoke with him in the late evening, to dreams of flowering trees in Wexford. We walked by the Seine. We knew we were utterly, utterly in love. Yet it was as though there was a wall in front of us. I said I was leaving the group. There was almost a grotesque look on Peter's face. He continued going to their meetings. He did not see the Finnish girl. I was writing a novel. One day he did not come back. He stayed away three days. I wished to kill myself not out of love for him but because I knew there'd be no other love. He returned. I knew he'd been with the girl. It was drawing near expiration time for his group. They were about to summon the forces of – of the Anti-Christ. I said goodbye to him. I walked to the Gard du Nord. Here, suitcase in my hand, before boarding the train I wished him dead. Peter's body was found in a small hotel which had burnt down some days later. There were roses outside, I saw by the newspaper photographs. I returned to Ireland. I told my friends who were Peter's friends I killed him but they said his death was an atonement, that the time had not yet come for the intended resurrection of the powers of evil, that there was still time to go. That time I suppose came with the first bombs on Notting Hill Gate. I became like a ghost during these years. I became unhappy and yet knew that my unhappiness was a source of possible reparation. I wished to speak to Peter again. There was no card in the tarot which would speak of him. And I had only myself to talk to. In time I held parties. Young men came to them and one called Alec I fell in love with. We went to Paris together. I conceived his child. The child was born mongoloid and died. I knew I should not have returned to this city. I went back to Wexford and there raised you, Catherine. There were times I made to speak to Peter. I could not contact him. In Paris now I know he will come. It is best I speak to the dead.'

She should have known the unholiness of the mission. Yet Aunt Madeleine had convinced herself of the exigencies of their affair, an affair which hung half-way between God and the Devil, an affair which included into its substance fat roses on spring days in Paris in the temporal haze before the war. 'I know,' Aunt Madeleine had said, 'that life is short. There are certain things within one's life one must guard like new unopened roses. Such was my affair with Peter. It was all such a terrible mistake, our dabbling in this magic. The young are wont to make mistakes. It seems like a dream now, the purpose of our séances in Gibraltar or Paris. But the real nightmare was in the human heart, the heart which couldn't distinguish and protect love when it had arrived.'

In Paris they'd made tracks to the house of a Russian woman with whom Aunt Madeleine had conversed. It had occurred to Catherine that they were taking part in more than a backward journey, this was the journey of a soul towards the point of its possession. She'd chosen cards from the tarot in the following days. Always the card of the hanged man had attained the most prominent place.

In their little hotel Catherine had studied Yeats, had read her aunt's novels and knew there were times in history that were irrevocably evil – such a time was her aunt's time. Aunt Madeleine unknowingly had slipped into dimensions of evil through an innocent affair. And the unfortunate succumbing to things supernatural, things dangerous.

Aunt Madeleine had arranged a séance with the Russian woman as medium. All the time the prominence of youth seemed to ride on her face. Catherine was frightened. She'd warned her aunt about it, her aunt had insisted. They'd entered a dark room. She needn't have taken part if she hadn't so desired but something in her had insisted. She'd desired to know the darkness of her roots, and the inability of extraordinary and innocent people like Aunt Madeleine to cope with their fates.

The baby was coming. It was pushing forward. Catherine's eyes opened. She thrilled to see Adoe, knowing her last sight of him had been in the garden before the baby had begun. His eyes sparkled, ingrained with copper points. She made to reach him, then saw Peter's face as she'd encountered it at that séance in Paris, collapsed writhing, screaming, until the density of hell seemed to burst from her.

Afterwards she'd struggled to know about such phenomena. In some séances it is reported that the medium can take the shape of the spirit she aspires to communicate with. This is called an ectoplasm. That evening in Paris such a strangeness had occurred. The Russian woman's face had transformed into Peter's ashen resemblance.

How much of what Aunt Madeleine had told her was true she'd never know. All she'd known was that Aunt Madeleine's involvement in evil had been greater than she'd admitted; love there may have been between her and Peter but her involvement in the group had been larger than she'd explained.

She'd been a high-priestess in this unfortunate cult. She'd cursed Peter when he'd sought to escape it.

She'd returned to Ireland on his death. Ever since, she'd tried to build a shrine of images, of actions to him in order to reach him again. These images, those actions, had accumulated in that ghastly séance in Paris when Catherine had screamed and her aunt had shot out of the door, shouting, 'I'm evil. I'm evil. I'm evil.'

The truth had emerged, laden with the horror of its homecoming. The ancestral castle had been the starting point in a European cult to aggravate the forces of evil, provoke them to a point of emergence whereby they could be harnessed. This plot was known to few, and poets like Yeats and young statesmen had visited the castle, knowing only its jovial side and the effulgence of its roses.

Catherine had never walked its paths again until she'd returned with Adoe. The facts about Aunt Madeleine she'd picked up in a witch hunt among Dublin elders. Aunt Madeleine had been incapacitated since that evening in Paris. When Catherine had taken an overdose of weedkiller in her final year at school, Aunt Madeleine had visited her in hospital, an ashen effigy. When she'd fallen in with a theatre group in Dublin to which Adoe had belonged, Aunt Madeleine had appeared, strictly forbidding her against men and especially those involved in theatre.

'They bring wounds,' she'd said, 'they bring your downfall.'

They'd been sitting in one of Bewleys' Oriental Cafés, when Catherine had noticed the tears in Aunt Madeleine's eyes and knew her to have repented. She'd been in love once. Wasn't that all you could judge her on? Peter had fallen in love with another woman, a Finnish girl belonging to a circus who had tried to persuade him away from a world of spirits, incantations and words about an apocalypse.

There had been an old man sitting behind Aunt Madeleine. Catherine had asked herself, 'How can I know about a generation other than my own? Above all how can I judge its torments, its fears, its movements – its indulgences?'

She'd been playing the young girl in *A Month in the Country*, her first main role, when she'd learnt Aunt Madeleine had died. It had been the time when yellow tulips would be nosing themselves unsuccessfully around the castle walls. Aunt Madeleine had passed away in her cottage. The funeral had taken place in Dublin. It had been a May day, a day of flowering horse-chestnut, a day of sunshine. Men of state had gathered, old men, ikons of Irish history. Catherine had wondered, perceiving the few men of literature, the men of state, how close to respectability and respectable quarters Aunt Madeleine's divinations had come?

An elderly gentleman with a beard turned to gold by acute rays of sunshine had read an oration. The puzzle was over. Catherine had turned away from the grave, the past was buried, save for the few intimations old men gave her of Aunt Madeleine's involvement or the questions asked of her by theatre people who presumed her to be an expert in the tarot.

Her eyes grazed with sunshine. She awoke. In front of her Adoe stood, he was holding a child. The child had his circuitous brown eyes. He bent, kissed her. She slept. This time her sleep was easier and her dreams wound with them a trail of January snowdrops, a smile of Aunt Madeleine's, one of those extraordinary smiles she gave when she'd made a sponge cake, iced it with caramel and recalled the vibrancy, the possibilities of being young, raven-haired and a woman of talent, of 'exceptional talent', as the blurbs read and the old men stuttered, over whiskeys, at literary parties or on the streets of Dublin, Paris, London a long time ago when fogs descended more easily and circumstances always seemed to point to a world, somewhere beyond our own.

JOSEPH HONE

The Captain in the Pipes

The Mossops had a problem: they were unhappy.

Henry Mossop had seen the Aer Lingus Fly-Drive advertisement in the *Telegraph* Colour Magazine and thought the unusual holiday offered might form a cure to their dumb distress. For that, as he saw it, was their problem: they had ceased to communicate. So he had gone into the travel agent in Plymouth that same day and booked two passages to Ireland forthwith.

The Mossops had never been to Ireland. But Henry, in the course of his career, had known a number of Irish people. They were a lively, talkative race. And this, together with the other friendly attributes of the country generally, he saw as an ideal tonic for their own awkward condition.

There was the change of life to consider, too, Henry thought: or rather, the fact that life hadn't changed. He was nearly forty – and Chief Communications Officer on a Type 42 Guided Missile Destroyer, HMS *Trent*. But his long-expected promotion to the same position on the carrier *Ark Royal* had not materialized and a sense of failure had begun to nibble at the edges of his soul. Their son Giles had been put down in a prep school near Tiverton; he had two weeks' leave coming up in October . . . Fresh fields, pastures new, Henry Mossop thought, as he left the travel agency.

Sheila Mossop wore fashionable, hexagonal-shaped spectacles but always squeezed the toothpaste from the very bottom of the tube. She too was nearly forty, with thin brown hair, cut short, coming in wisps over her ears – rather a small and decided person, yet not a mousy woman, though latterly she had come to see herself as such. In fact she was bright and forthcoming by nature. But these qualities were largely dormant in her now.

Her problem was not one of communication with her husband. She sometimes thought he talked too much, in fact. She had simply wanted a larger family – something to extend and occupy herself with during her husband's many absences: she had wanted a *proper* family, she had always told herself, a bunch of children growing up like flowers all round her. But Henry, she had long ago realized, lacked adventure in that direction. He had been parsimonious in bed to begin with, afterwards miserly – and finally his lovemaking had become quite bankrupt. She had tried several times to resuscitate the currency with him but without success, for she was shy and inexperienced in such matters. And though she forgot this failure now in her day-to-day affairs, she nursed the hurt obscurely deep inside her.

Henry, on the other hand, viewed the problem differently: he believed that his wife had become frigid. Though he was sensible enough, as he saw it, to regard this as a natural misfortune and not a fault of either of theirs. It was a disability concomitant with the approach of middle age and a flaw in English women generally, he felt.

An old friend and former shipmate of his, who served aboard the *QE2*, whom he had consulted about the problem some months previously, had tactfully intimated that he should force himself upon his wife. 'It's the only way – in the circumstances,' he had said, before buying another round of gin and tonics at the local golf club – large ones this time.

Henry found himself thinking about this advice as they drove down from Dublin in their hired car – delayed by a large herd of cows just outside a town called Naas on the main road to Cork. The animals wobbled their udders and jostled their big brown backsides against the side of the car, squeezing past the bumpers. No, Henry thought with disgust – I cannot rape her. His friend's advice, he decided – though possibly suited to some of the passengers aboard the *QE2* – was not a course of action open to an officer in Her Majesty's Senior Service.

They drove on, in silence, across the long rolling countryside, on an almost empty main road, the sun beginning to dip from a cloudless blue sky. The weather, Henry thought, was unseemly for the country and the time of year. It had been a very hot day.

The hotel, a small four-square early Victorian building which had once been a rectory, lay a mile outside Kinsale – on a hill above the small fishing port where black and white terraced cottages ran down to the quay with several smart hotels along it, for the place was a busy and popular tourist resort during the summer season. But now, in mid-October, it had reverted to its ancient ways: a few elderly figures walked the quiet back streets up the hill; a trawler made ready for sea; a family packed up their car in front of the hotel, down from Cork for the day.

The view from the hotel was calm and beautiful in the last of the sunlight. The Mossops, having unpacked and dressed for dinner, sat next to the big bow window in the drawing room sipping Tio Pepe. It was a pleasant room, like that of a private house, with deep chintz armchairs, hunting prints, together with a restrained Russell Flint reproduction over the mantelpiece entitled 'Persian Market'. They looked out at the long, grey-blue swell of the Atlantic beyond the headland to their right. Calm as a millpond, Henry thought contentedly. He sipped his sherry again and put the glass down carefully. The little round table between them was antique, done in highly polished rosewood.

There was no bar in the hotel. But drinks were readily available to residents, Mrs Jackson, the proprietress, had told Henry on arrival. Meanwhile, the sherry came with the compliments of the house, she had added sweetly.

Henry remembered her smile. It had been a strange thing – warm and full, yet somehow set like a transparency over a sad face. Sixtyish, he thought – genteel Irish with a soft southern burr in her voice and an abundant flow of hair, so healthy-looking that he had been surprised at its complete whiteness, an unnatural white, like a powdered eighteenth-century wig. There was something sensuous and attractive about her, Henry decided. But he couldn't exactly identify it. Perhaps it was the way she walked – very lightly, delicately, like a young woman tiptoeing to bed. And she had deep blue eyes, unclouded still – like a girl's too – which she looked directly at you with, as if issuing a slightly risqué invitation. He mentioned this fact to Sheila.

'Yes,' she replied. 'She speaks with her eyes – and listens with them as well. But why Jackson? That's not an Irish name is it?' They sipped their sherry in silence, pondering this fact.

Shortly afterwards they heard brisk footsteps outside on the gravel and saw an elderly, rather angry-looking man stomping past the bow-window. He was dressed in a heavy blue windcheater and stout hiker's boots with plus-fours – though neither the weather nor the ground under-foot merited such accessories. He disappeared from view and they heard the hall door open sharply, the draught flap grating abrasively across the floor.

They were surprised when this brusque entry was not followed by any sound of movement in the hall, nor by the door closing again. The Mossops looked at each other and then out of the window. But the view was empty.

They were startled when they turned back to see the man standing behind them in his stockinged feet, holding his boots in one hand.

He was very small, they noticed now – hardly more than five feet in his socks – his face badly weather-beaten, the skin shrunk against the bones, dark and leathery as the Tollund Man. A large pair of old naval binoculars hung from his neck. His ears were too big for his head and the lobes drooped noticeably: his sparse hair was parted on the left and combed severely sideways in the old fashion. He breathed heavily, his little ferret blue eyes gleaming at them in outraged curiosity. Despite his diminutive size he exuded dominance. It was as if two large men had just come into the room and not one small one.

'Good evening,' he said, coming towards them. 'You'll be the Mossops.' He held his one free hand out. 'Captain Jackson.'

Henry stood up automatically, as if back on board ship.

'Good evening, sir. Henry Mossop. And this is my wife, Sheila.'

The Captain took her hand, held it for some long seconds, looking at her appraisingly. 'Very nice indeed,' he said at last. 'Let me join you for a drink as soon as I'm out of these togs.' He looked at the sunset through the bow window, the shadows settling gently over the sea and the village below them. 'Well below the yardarm,' he remarked. Then he turned back to Mrs Mossop. 'Going to be a change though. Glass is falling.' He looked back out over the bay. 'Can't see the Old Head. Always means a change.' Then he turned to Henry. 'Good trip? From Plymouth – saw from your booking. Needn't ask, need I? – saw it at once. Navy man, eh?'

'Yes, sir. The *Trent*. Communications officer – '

But the Captain had turned away. 'Won't be a moment.'

Then he turned back. 'The *Trent*? Guided Missile Destroyer?'

'Yes, sir.'

'Well done. Was with the *Prince of Wales* myself.' The Captain left the room.

'The *Prince of Wales*?' Sheila asked.

'Yes. Battlecruiser. The last war. Went down with half her crew off Singapore in 1942.'

'How strange.'

'Yes. Don't suppose it was his fault.'

'No. I meant – him, being married to Mrs Jackson.'

'Yes.'

They sipped their sherry once more and pondered this fact.

The tapping started that night.

The Mossops' room gave out directly southwards, looking over the rim of the headland straight down to the Atlantic. They had gone to bed early, leaving their bedroom window slightly open, for it had been a warm day and the room still retained a lot of the heat. It was this which puzzled Henry when he woke, some time after midnight – the fact that the central heating had suddenly come on in the middle of the night, in warm weather, for the tapping came from the radiator just beneath the window.

He lay there, half asleep, listening to the confused medley of taps and groans – the water coursing through the system, warming the boards and metal and making them creak, just as his own central heating behaved in Plymouth when it was started up from cold. He drifted off to sleep again.

The tapping noise was louder and more regular when

he woke a second time. And since he was warm enough already he decided to turn the radiator off, thus getting rid of the noise at the same time.

He got out of bed and touched the metal ribbing. It was stone cold. And the tap at the bottom was already firmly turned off. Looking out of the window he noticed that a wind was starting to blow strongly from the south-west, rustling the curtains. He could hear the distant thud of waves now, the huge Atlantic breakers falling on the headland in the dark night. The Captain's forecast had been correct: the weather was brewing up. He shut the window and went back to bed.

Just as he lay down he realized something was wrong. His long experience in naval communications alerted him, some sixth sense warning him before he could identify the source of his unease.

Then he recognized it – the tapping coming strongly from the radiator now: three taps, then three with longer intervals; three more short ones. A pause, before the sequence was repeated.

Henry sat up in bed. There was no doubt about it. An S-O-S signal was coming through the pipes in morse. A Mayday call.

His first thought was that the Captain might be playing some elaborate joke on him – tapping the central heating pipes somewhere downstairs. Henry thought he recognized the sort of man: a retired naval hearty, gone to seed in the wilds of Ireland, up to some prank with an imagined fellow spirit. But as he listened to the continuous cry for help rattling through the pipes Henry began to doubt this. The joke was too elaborate – and too serious. Henry's morse was a little rusty but he soon picked up the drift of the message.

'S-O-S- S-S I-N-V-E-R-N-E-S-S L-A-T-5-1.3-4-N L-O-N-8.3-2-W   B-O-I-L-E-R-G-O-N-E-R-E-A-R-H-O-L-D-F-I-L-L . . .'

Henry jumped out of bed and turned his side light on. Sheila woke in the next bed and began to mumble something. But by then Henry was scrabbling about in his jacket looking for paper and something to write with.

'What's happened?' Sheila asked, calmly, in a way that Henry had come to hate.

'Wait – quiet!' Henry got a chair and sat next to the radiator where he started to take down the message. The tapping had become less coherent now, more hurried.

'A-B-O-T T-O A-B-A-N-D-O-N S-H-I L-A-T-1.3-4-N . . .'

'Are you mad?' Sheila went on, sitting up in bed.

'Shshsh,' he said. But the tapping stopped just then.

'Without thinking, so drawn was he by the urgency of the event, Henry began to tap a message back, using his pen as a morse key on top of the radiator.

'R-E-C-E-I-V-I-N-G Y-O-U A-T K-I-N-S-A-L-E R-E-P-E-A-T P-O-S-I-T-I-O-N A-R-E Y-O-U R-E-C-E-I-V-I-N-G M-E . . .'

But there was silence then. The noises had quite stopped.

'Henry, do get get back to bed. What's wrong? What is it?'

'It's a message, don't you see.' He turned to her, amazed at her lack of concern. 'The ship is sinking.'

'Nonsense. It's just the radiator.'

Just then it started to go again, but faintly now.

'S-O-S A-B-A-N-D-O-N-I-N-G S-H-I-P L-A-S-T P-O-S L-A-T-5-1.3-4-N L-O-N-8.3-2-W S-O-S . . .' The tapping suddenly stopped.

'Do come back to *bed*,' Sheila said rather petulantly. Henry looked at her, his lips quivering with excitement and enmity.

* * *

'Just some quirk in the central heating,' Sheila said to him next morning at breakfast. 'Some bizarre electrical disturbance. The storm last night perhaps – a ship somewhere out there.'

'We listened to the Irish news this morning. And the BBC. There was nothing – no reports of any ship sinking. And how can it have been a quirk in the central heating? The heating wasn't on.' Henry ate another sausage. He felt nervous, elated – for the first time in years: a feeling he'd last remembered properly when he had read about Gagool the Witchfinder in *King Solomon's Mines* as a child. Henry felt childish suddenly. For of course, on the surface, the whole thing did seem ridiculous and impossible. On the surface. Yet on the other hand he had heard the message, had written it down . . . Henry sipped his coffee silently, thinking. He looked up. Sheila was saying something. He hadn't heard her.

'Do wake up, Henry.'

'I'm sorry.'

'I said, "I like it here. It's a lovely place."' She looked at him with tenderness, for the first time in months. But he didn't notice it.

After breakfast, while Sheila was upstairs getting ready to go out for a walk with him, Henry wandered into the hall. Above a big blue glazed porcelain umbrella stand and next to a large barometer, he found himself gazing at a framed marine chart, covering south-west Ireland. His eye caught the latitude line of 51 north – and then the longitude 8 west. Allowing for the extra degrees on each line which he had received in the messages the previous night, he made a rough visual transfix on the chart, running one index finger north, the other westwards. The lines bisected each other on a spot about five or ten miles out to sea, directly south of the Old Head of Kinsale. Henry felt the skin around his shoulders prickle. At the same moment he became aware of someone standing behind him. He turned.

The Captain was looking over his shoulder – or trying to, for he was in his stockinged feet again, holding his boots in one hand.

'Morning,' he said breezily. 'In for a spell of bad weather. Glass's still dropping. Quite a rough stretch of coast, this, when it blows. Don't suppose you know it. Navy doesn't come to these parts any more. Though they used to, of course. We had a base in Cobh before the war. Queenstown it was then. Lot of Admiralty dependents still live around here. *Lusitania* went down off the Old Head in 1915. Brought the Yanks in. Lot of wrecks . . .'

'Yes.' Henry turned. He decided not to tell the Captain about the tapping in the radiator. It might seem stupid. On the other hand it would do no harm to ask him about the ship itself. The Captain, after all, had given him a natural opening.

'Yes,' Henry went on, 'I seem to remember a ship – the *Inverness*, wasn't it? – went down near here.'

There was silence. The Captain licked his dry lips.

'The *Inverness*? Hadn't heard of it. Not in my time. There was the *Loch Tay* in '37. And a German coaster, the *Bremerhaven*, the same year. And during the war, of course, quite a few others. But not the *Inverness*, as far as I know. Why do you ask?'

'Oh, I heard about it – an Irishman on the *Trent*. He had a relation . . .' Henry let the words die away, embarrassed at his lie.

The Captain made a dry, crackling noise, the sound rising from deep within his throat. Henry thought he was laughing. But he was simply trying to coax some phlegm up. The Captain humphed vigorously several times before moving away.

*   *   *

The sky was fairly clear but it was very windy when they went out, with white horses scudding all over the angry grey sea beyond the fishing port. Henry had brought his own binoculars with him and together they walked through the village and up the far side of the valley and along the grassy promontory towards the Old Head. From here, beyond the ruins of what looked like an old army barracks on the cliff, Henry gazed out to sea, swinging his glasses widely over the whole stormy vision. A small trawler was making heavy progress, running against the tide for shelter, riding the waves like a car on a roller coaster, sometimes barely moving at all against the huge swell.

Sheila was cold. 'What are you looking at? Let's go back.'

'That ship – it must have been like this. Out there.'

'Damn that ship. Aren't we having a holiday – away from all that?'

'Yes. I'm sorry.' They turned back.

But the mystery of the SS *Inverness* continued to hang in Henry's mind like the sword of Damocles all morning. He felt he had behaved unprofessionally about it. Shouldn't he at least have told someone about the messages? Then he reminded himself again that the whole thing was impossible: no ship could communicate through a central heating system; no one would have believed him.

None the less, the incident continued to agitate him. So that, when they stopped for coffee at the Trident Hotel on the quay on their way back, Henry decided to telephone a friend of his, a fellow officer on the *Trent*, whom he knew to be currently on shore leave in Plymouth. He gave the man details of the message and asked him to check with Lloyds Shipping Register in London and call him back at his own hotel that evening if he came up with anything. Sheila looked at him with sour incomprehension when he returned from the telephone booth.

Before lunch, upstairs in the bedroom of their own hotel, Henry saw the Captain standing at the end of the small rose garden, looking over the last of the wind-blown petals, gazing out to sea with his glasses. Getting his own binoculars out again, while Sheila was in the bathroom, Henry followed the Captain's line of vision. But there was nothing out to sea except the tossed spume rising in white drifts from the violent water.

The Captain didn't join them for a drink that evening. He had a fluey cold, Mrs Jackson said, and was trying to kill it quickly upstairs in bed with whiskey and lemon. Mrs Jackson looked tired, her attitude preoccupied, even unhappy. Apart from the few other guests, she had her hands full with the Captain as well, she seemed to imply, hurrying about between the reception desk, the kitchen behind, and their bedroom upstairs.

At seven o'clock Henry's friend in Plymouth telephoned. Henry took the call in a little cabin at the end of the hall, closing the door firmly behind him. His friend had most of the details to hand. He read them out, the line crackling with static, and Henry jotted the information down on a pad supplied by a firm of bottlers in Cork.

'. . . the SS *Inverness*, a 3,000-ton cargo steamer, launched at Clydeside in 1912, originally owned by the North British Transport and Trading Company in Edinburgh, sold to the Irish Shipping Lines in 1930 – had sunk with the loss of half her crew on the night of 9 October 1932 five miles off the Old Head of Kinsale, on a voyage with mixed cargo from Cardiff to Galway. Reports from the few survivors confirmed the Mayday messages received at the time: the ship's boiler had sprung a leak in heavy weather and had subsequently exploded. The boat had sunk shortly afterwards, going down stern first, the rear section badly holed beneath the waterline. The Master of the ship, who had not survived, was a Captain Patrick Hennessy of Irish Shipping Lines . . .'

When Henry returned to the drawing room Sheila wasn't there. He found her upstairs crying in their bedroom.

'I'm sorry,' he said, sitting down beside her and trying to console her. 'I won't go on with it all. But I had to find out about it. Can't you see? I had to.'

'*Damn* that ship,' Sheila gasped through her tears. 'Damn all your ships.' She stood up to get a handkerchief. Then, in the silence the moment before she blew her nose, they both turned in horror to the window. The radiator had started to tap again. Henry went over to it.

'It's all right,' he said, smiling at her with relief. 'This time it really is the heating. It's on. The maid must have done it when she came to turn down our beds. Don't worry. It's not another message.'

But Henry lied. Though the radiator had indeed been turned on, the tapping was another message. He heard the first of it: '. . . T-A-I-N H-E-N-N-E-S-S-Y A-R-E Y-O-U R-E-C-E-I-V-I-N-G . . .' But by then Henry had shepherded his wife quickly out of the room and down to dinner.

They shared a bottle of light Beaujolais with their steak and afterwards Sheila slept more soundly than usual. But Henry found sleep impossible. The radiator had remained quite silent. But he was sure it would start up again. And when it didn't he felt disappointed.

Sometime before midnight, however – the wind getting up outside and the sea booming strongly again in the distance – he heard a slow drip of water coming from the window. When he got up to investigate he found the tap at the bottom of the radiator was leaking slightly. He put his fingers round it, staunching the drops, and at once the morse started again. It came in spurts but faded right away when ever Henry took his hand off the pipe, so that he had to bind the tap with a handkerchief before he could make any sense of the message. What he heard made his shoulderblades prickle.

'. . . he was at Cobh, you see – Jackson, with the Admiralty, in 1931 – just after I took over the *Inverness*, Mary and I were living in Cork then . . .' The message began to fade. Henry pressed his fingers hard against the handkerchief and it came back again. '. . . met her at a naval reception – and when she was shopping – came round to see us – he had something . . .' The morse here became confused, almost frantic, and Henry could no longer follow it. Gradually it cleared again. '. . . when I took over the Cardiff–Galway run I knew he was with her – that was the end of . . .' The message became incoherent again, slowly fading. Then, after about half a minute, the original Mayday message came back very strongly: 'S-O-S . . . S-O-S . . .' Then there was silence.

Henry took his hand off the pipe. Rain beat on the window above him, the storm gathering strength from the south-west. A window or a door slammed somewhere outside and he crouched in the darkness of the bedroom as if shielding himself from the weather. Jackson, he thought, with the Admiralty in Cobh in 1931: and Captain Jackson with his Irish wife – or rather, as it appeared, with Captain Hennessy's wife – retired in Kinsale forty-five years later. Was that how it was? And if so, how could he help? What help was there for an infidelity so old and a long-drowned sailor complaining in the night? Henry found himself disbelieving the whole thing for a minute – until he remembered his conversation with the

Captain in the hall about the *Inverness*. That was real enough, as had been the Captain's denial that he knew anything about the ship. If the Captain in the pipes was right, Henry thought, Jackson must see him now as some live ghost come to haunt him all the way from Plymouth.

A plumber came from the village next morning to repair the leaking radiator. While the man was in his bedroom Henry – mentioning his qualifications and anxious to look over the system for himself – offered to help him check the central heating installation downstairs: perhaps something was wrong with the electrical circuits in the time switch, for he had explained to the plumber the uneven performance of this mechanism.

The boiler was housed down some wooden steps in a small basement beneath the kitchen. The room smelt of burnt oil and oily tools, like the engine room of a ship Henry thought. There was a neat row of spanners and other engineering equipment above a work bench to one side and some old cabin trunks piled up in one corner. Henry suddenly noticed the white lettering on one of them: 'Lt A. P. C. Jackson, Admiralty Buildings, Section 17/F, Queenstown, Co. Cork, IRELAND.

Together they looked over the time switch above the boiler. Then they unscrewed the cowling next to the chimney and tested the hot water thermostat beneath; finally they removed the igniter and tested it. Everything seemed in perfect order. The plumber went upstairs to check the electric pump in the main hot press, while Henry remained below to activate the time switch, thus giving the whole system a complete test. On a signal from above he threw the switch and the boiler came to life with a soft roar. It had not been in operation for more than a minute when Henry noticed a small leak in the cold water input pipe. It wasn't much, just a dribble beneath the

control tap. But the colour was strange, a red colour.
Rust, Henry thought, as he wiped his hands, hearing the
plumber coming down the steps again. But it wasn't the
plumber. It was Captain Jackson.

'Spot of trouble?' he asked from the stairway, dressed
in an old paisley dressing-gown and slippers.

'Not really. Just a small leak in the cold pipe from
upstairs. I thought maybe I could help over the electrics –
thought the circuits might be out. But they're okay.'

'Kind of you to lend a hand.' The Captain took a large
spanner from above the work bench and came towards
Henry, who stepped back involuntarily. The boiler was
roaring now and the temperature was beginning to rise in
the confined space. The Captain brandished the spanner,
enhancing his grip on it. Henry readied himself. But the
little man moved away from him at the last moment and
bent down to one side of the boiler where he started to
tighten – or loosen – the large nut on the input valve.

'Gets clogged up after the summer, not being used,' he
said. But he failed to make much headway in his work.
As he bent down, however, the collar of his dressing-
gown pulled back and Henry noticed a series of neat little
red indentations running across his neck. Teeth marks –
love bites? Henry wondered.

The Captain stood up. 'There. That'll do it.'

But he had not done it. The drip continued
undiminished.

'Full steam ahead, eh?' The Captain's eyes twinkled in
the gloomy light and he looked at Henry mischievously.

Just then, before Henry could make any suitable
response, a loud tapping noise came from the input pipe,
from the valve which the Captain had been tending. It
was morse again, Henry realized at once. 'B-A-S-T-A-R
. . .' But he lost the rest of it, for the Captain immediately

picked up the spanner again and gave the pipe a resound-
ing clout with it. 'Bloody pipes,' he said, putting the
spanner back carefully in its allotted pouch above the
work bench. The noise stopped abruptly. But the leak
didn't.

It was Sheila's bath late that night which brought things
to a head: her scream half-way through washing. She was
looking at the taps when Henry arrived from the bedroom, sitting bolt upright in the water, rubbing her hands,
her face creased with fear and pain.

'What happened?'

'The tap . . .'

Henry moved to put his hand on it. 'Don't!' she
shrieked. 'It's live. It's electric. I just touched it.'

'Nonsense, Sheila.'

'It *is* you fool. It's live.'

'All right. Don't shout. Just get out of the water –
carefully.'

Sheila got out, wrapping a towel prudishly around her.
Henry got one of his pipe cleaners from the next room.
Then, exposing the metal core at one end and pushing the
other into the rubber heel of his shoe, he brushed the tap
lightly with the metal. A jagged blue spark sizzled
between the two extremities.

'My God,' Henry said. 'I'll get the Captain. This is
crazy.'

Turning to leave the bathroom, he heard the cistern
above the lavatory warbling gently and the noise of water
trickling fast down the sides of the bowl. Then he noticed
that, instead of draining away, the level of the water in
the pan beneath was slowly rising. Sheila followed his
glance. She came to him, fearful – the towel dropping
away from her, holding to him, embracing him almost.

'Let's get away from here, darling. Right away. There's something wrong. Please!'

He held her for a moment before shepherding her gently into the bedroom. 'How can we? It's the middle of the night. We'll get another room.'

He didn't push her away. Instead she fell from his arms in disappointment, collapsing on her bed. The moment's reconciliation had been lost.

'I'll get the Captain,' Henry said. The weather was blowing up once more outside, another night storm running in from the Atlantic. 'Stay here. Don't move. Don't *touch* anything,' he said, before going out on to the landing, closing the bedroom door carefully behind him.

The passage-way was dark. The hotel slept. But he thought he knew where the Jacksons' private rooms were – up a small stairway at the end of the landing. He knocked quite loudly on an un-numbered door.

'What is it?' a voice said petulantly after some moments.

'It's Mossop. Can I see you? It's urgent – I'm sorry to – '

The door opened abruptly. Captain Jackson glowered at him, a minute and angry figure in his paisley dressing-gown and stockinged feet. Henry explained. The Captain humphed. 'We'll take a look downstairs then. Shut off the electrics. Can you give me a hand? Your line of country.'

Henry didn't want to go with him but the Captain was already herding him down the passage-way. In the kitchen he picked up a big torch. The wind was buffeting the windows furiously now, shaking the whole house. But the roar from the boiler immediately beneath them seemed louder still, unnaturally loud. The Captain opened the door to the basement and they moved down the steps. The heat was intense. The metal cowling above the boiler shimmered and there was a large pool of water beneath the main input pipe. The valve was leaking badly now. Henry went forward.

'You'll have to turn everything off,' he shouted. 'Have you got some candles for upstairs?' He turned. The Captain had disappeared.

The door at the head of the steps was just closing. Henry heard the key turning in the lock as he rushed up towards it. He hammered on it furiously. Then he heard the Captain's voice – vigorous, brutal.

'Two can play at this game, Mossop. Getting me up in the middle of the night with your bloody tricks, are you now? Oh, don't think I don't know what you're up to! Come to plague me about the *Inverness*, tapping out morse on the central heating pipes every evening. And you were down here this morning tampering with the system. Well, now you've messed the whole thing up – you can just stay there with it and cool your heels.'

Henry heard him move away. He went back down the steps. The cowling round the bottom of the boiler, where the oil-feed was, had begun to glow and the leak in the input pipe was really running now, the blood-red water seeping across the floor towards him. Henry grabbed the big spanner before running back up the stairs and attacking the stout door viciously with it.

Mary Jackson had woken with the knocking ten minutes before and now she felt cold – the wind and rain whipping at the windows, the full angry force of an Atlantic gale storming the house. She leant over to the side of her high bed and turned her electric blanket on.

A moment after her hand had moved the switch, she arched herself in a fearful spasm, as though the mattress had become a bed of nails. Her head knocked violently against the bed-head as the voltage struck her, coursing through her limbs, making her whole body tremble for a moment, as if at the apex of some great pleasure. Then she lay back, quite still, taking to death like the little death of love.

As the Captain came up the stairs he saw that one of the central heating pipes that ran along the landing skirting board had sprung a leak, the water spraying out in an arc above him, the edges of it spattering his face. He held on to the banisters for a moment, undecided. The house thudded and banged and seemed to move in the big wind, to list and dive in the storm. Then, ducking through the spray, shielding his face, he went purposefully forward.

When he opened their bedroom door he saw his wife looking at him, her head twisted sideways on the pillow, lips slightly open. He thought she was about to say something to him – something angry, for from a distance her expression seemed annoyed. But when he came closer he saw that she had been gazing straight through him with a frozen expression of awful pain.

He thought she might still be alive and could be resuscitated with the kiss of life. He forgot his damp hands and face and didn't notice his wife's arm still lying across the electric cord, so that when he bent over her and put his lips to hers, his whole body shuddered and convulsed, as hers had done, in a brief but violent agony. He fell across her on the bed, joining her inseparably in a last embrace.

In the Mossops' bedroom the lavatory bowl had over-flowed and the water by now had risen half an inch over the bathroom floor and begun to trickle out into the bedroom, swamping the fitted carpet. Sheila Mossop sat with her feet upon the bed, as it if were a raft, and watched the water soak across the room, forming a moat between her and the door. She was afraid to move –

afraid to step in the water, or to touch the metal door handle and escape out on to the landing. She sat there listening to the fearful wind and, when the lights in the bedroom suddenly went out and some moments after one of the windows blew open in a ferocious gust, she screamed. She stayed where she was for some moments, The wind and rain streaming across the room and the curtains flapping like pistol shots. No one heeded her screams and since there was no water on that side of the bed she put her feet down gingerly and went over to try and close the window.

Walking towards it, pressing against the wind, she put her hand out into the darkness, searching for the window clasp. Instead she touched something damp and soft. The next moment the curtain had wrapped itself round her shoulders, the material slapping viciously about her breasts. She tried to disentangle herself from it. But, before she could do so, the storm grasped her and pushed her backwards into the room – so violently that the curtain was torn from its runners and she fell, hitting her head on the floor.

She lay there stunned for a minute and when her mind cleared she gazed up into the blackness with relief. Henry had come back. She couldn't see him in the darkness but she could hear footsteps. He was walking over by the window, trying to close it, she thought. She propped herself up on one arm, rubbing the back of her head.

'Henry? Thank God. I'm here – by the bed. I fell . . .'

There was no reply. She heard the squeak of some kind of abrasive clothing – a mackintosh or oilskin – as the footsteps left the window without closing it and approached her.

'Henry?'

Now she was terrified but she could no longer scream. Instead she fought, blindly, as the elements of wind and rain seemed to burst above her now, falling on her, pinning her to the floor. Her nightdress whipped up her legs as she struggled – yet vainly struggled, for what she felt above her, pressing down on her, had no body, no substance – was simply a weightless force which she could not touch, nor rid herself of, yet which possessed her fully and with pain. Her arms and thighs ached with it – and with the struggle she made to escape, turning first one way and then the other. Finally she ceased the fight and gave herself to the strange agony.

When Henry found her she was lying half naked on the floor, the beam of Captain Jackson's big torch spotlighting her like the victim of some hit and run accident, the curtain pulled harshly round her neck and down her midriff. He put the torch on the bed and lifted her up, a bundle of damp flesh, her head lolling back over his arm. He thought her dead. But when he laid her flat and rubbed her body and started to resuscitate her mouth-to-mouth, she regained consciousness rapidly and began to struggle with him violently, pushing him away.

'Get dressed, then,' he said rather abruptly. 'Quickly. We're getting out.' They could hear the few other guests outside on the landing now, moving down the stairs, evacuating the building. Henry managed to get her into her dressing-gown. Then, grabbing a few of their things and shoving them in a suitcase, he helped her across the swamped carpet and out on to the landing. Here it was wetter still and they moved down the stairs after the others through a rainfall of water. It sprayed from pipes above the skirting boards, streamed from radiators, leaked from ceilings, and when they got down to the hall they had to paddle through the water, several inches deep by the reception desk.

'What about the Captain and his wife?' someone

shouted from the darkness outside as Henry and Sheila hurried forward, the last to leave as they thought. Henry turned and shone the torch back as they got to the hall door. The water was flowing down the stairs and for an instant Henry saw the Captain standing on the half-landing, an exultant figure in a naval cap and oilskins, holding firmly on to the banisters as though on to a swaying bridge, like a mad man happily sinking with his ship. He was just about to go back for him when the explosion rocked him forward, pushing them both out into the night. The boiler had gone up.

Outside, stumbling on to the gravel drive, they saw the back of the building, where the kitchens were, spurt with flame as the fire caught on, feeding on the oil supply. Soon all that part of the hotel was ablaze, rafters and slates falling to the ground, while the front of the house smouldered damply against the flames.

Late next morning, in the Trident Hotel down on the quay, Henry looked from their bedroom window up the hill to where the now completely gutted building smoked like a hulk on the horizon. Sheila lay asleep, under sedation, across the room from him. But her hysterical words, before the doctor had come, remained very much alive in him. 'Rape,' she had screamed, among many other bitter things, years of repressed resentment exploding in her. 'I wonder you hadn't thought of that before.'

'But I wasn't *in* the room, Sheila,' he'd replied. 'It was the curtain – round your neck.'

And he had believed this until afterwards, when the detective from Cork had questioned him downstairs, and told him during the course of their interview that both Captain Jackson and his wife had been found dead in their bedroom.

'In an oilskin – and naval cap?' Henry had asked.

'No. Just in his dressing-gown. Why do you ask?'

'Oh, nothing,' Henry said.

'Did you see anybody?' the detective went on, encouraged. 'Any stranger in or around the hotel last night?'

'No,' Henry lied. 'Why?'

'Well, we have to treat all this as deliberate, I'm afraid. Arson.'

'I don't understand?'

'The Provisionals. The Provisional IRA,' the man said apologetically. 'There've been several other cases recently. Various threats – and attacks on retired British people living over here. Especially from the forces.'

'Oh, yes. I see,' Henry said. 'It's a bad business.'

'Indeed,' the detective agreed. 'A long, bad business. I'm sorry for your trouble.'

JENNIFER JOHNSTON

The Theft

I feel I have to write this down as an explanation of sorts,
not that there is anyone remaining who will care much or
ask any questions, apart from the authorities and possibly
the amiable Mr Moriarty. I am sorry about Mr Moriarty's
involvement, but he has been well paid for any inconven-
ience that he may have to suffer.

It is the 19th of June and we seem to be having one of
those spells of beautiful weather that I remember so well
as a child. The air is still and golden and warm. It is
coming on for evening now and the rays of the sun slant
past my window and cast long, graceful shadows on the
grass. In the distance someone is cutting grass with one of
those old-fashioned machines that whirrs as you push it
along, rather than roars. The small garden of the hotel is
neat below my window, straight rows of flowers parade in
their beds, no weeds provoke the eye. I have asked Mr
Moriarty to collect me and take me once more to Beauregard when he has had his tea, a meal they eat in this
country around the hour of six, so I have not much time.

I was born in Beauregard in Co. Cork on this date
eighty-five years ago.

Life was very different then to the way it has become
today. That has all been said before. Each generation
looks back with regret. 'Things were so much better then,'
they sigh. People will never be so brilliant, the sun will
never shine as it did then, time, which always seemed to
stop at our command, no longer pays heed to our frantic
words. I have never been a person for looking over my

shoulder, but I remember the simple happinesses of childhood, and always in the back of my mind has been the memory of the unease that drove me at the age of nineteen from Beauregard and which now has drawn me back after all those innumerable years. I don't suppose my childhood was more idyllic than that of any other child brought up in similar circumstances. There may have been bad moments, hours, days, but the mind suppresses them.

I was an only child and passed most of my time, when not being taught, with one of my parents or the other. I grew to be impatient of the children who were invited, from time to time, to keep me company. I despised their chatter, their roughness, their lack of ideas. In short, I was a prig, and, I suppose, may have remained one ever since. Such friends as I have collected through my life became my friends because of the active searching quality of my mind, rather than the warmth of my personality. I digress, seeking perhaps to put off the moment when I must go. I must settle down and tell the story.

One spring afternoon, not long before my tenth birthday, it must have been about the turn of the century. I was sitting alone in the drawing room totally engrossed in a puzzle, that my mother had, not long before, spilled on to a table from a large linen bag. It was warm for May and two of the long south-facing windows were open on to the flagged terrace that ran the length of the drawing room a few feet above the level of the lawn. I had my back to the windows and the sun was warm on my head and shoulders as I leant, concentrating, over the table. I heard no sound, but suddenly became aware of the fact that I was being closely watched. I looked up, with a certain irritation, across the table to see a child of about my own age standing, staring at me. Her appearance was vaguely familiar to me, but I had no idea who she might be.

'Good afternoon,' I said. 'Did you come in through the window?'

She didn't reply.

'Is your mother with you?'

No word.

I fitted another piece into the puzzle before speaking to her again.

'I don't think I remember who you are. What is your name?'

She stared with a certain unfriendliness at me. She remained silent.

Obviously recognizing something of myself in her, I smiled grudgingly. 'You can help me do this puzzle if you like.'

She moved towards me and then with an abrupt gesture she leant across the table, scattering the pieces that I had so carefully assembled, and snatched something from beside me. I looked down to see what it was that she had taken and then quickly up, to give her a piece of my mind, but she had gone. The room was empty.

'Come back,' I called. 'Bring it back.'

There was no sound of running feet, no laughter, no rustle of skirts. There was only silence and from the distance the regular click, click, of one of the gardeners clipping a hedge. I got up and went to the window and looked out. There was no one to be seen.

'Do come back.' My voice was filled with anxiety.

I ran back to the table to try and discover what she had taken. The pieces of the puzzle were scattered on the table top and some had spilled on to the floor. There had been nothing else there, nothing to take. I burst into sudden tears. A short while later my mother came into the room and found me crying.

'My darling,' she said with anxiety. 'Whatever is the matter?'

'She took it,' I sobbed.

'Who took it, darling? Who took what?'

'I don't know.'

Sudden hysteria was making my voice shrill. She took my hands in hers, her cool fingers pressing into my skin.

'Darling, stop. Do stop. There's a good girl. Explain. Just explain.'

I tried to stop crying. I tried to speak to her in a coherent voice. My hands in her hands trembled.

'She came in and she took it.'

'She took what, child?'

I shook my head.

'I don't know what she took, but she stood there.'

I pointed to the spot on the other side of the table where the child had been standing looking at me.

'She took something.'

I began to cry again. I had lost something. I had no idea what it was that I had lost, but I was filled with outrage that anyone should treat me as the strange child had done.

My mother looked mildly alarmed. She went to the window and then out on to the terrace. There was obviously no child to be seen anywhere.

'What did she look like?'

She came back into the room and put a hand on my head, smoothing gently at my hair. She was a very gentle woman and her movements were always graceful and considered.

I described the girl to her. She handed me her handkerchief and smiled. 'Come, dry your eyes. A little moment of the imagination. It happens to many people. Fancy. A little air, my darling, will do us both good. Come.' She took my hand and we went out into the sun. The occurrence was never mentioned again.

The matter slipped, after a few days into the back of

my own mind and quite soon I forgot about the child altogether. We moved through summer and the golden autumn and then Christmas with its amazing excitements was there. On Christmas Eve the gardener and two of his men would carry the tall tree into the drawing room. It would be put standing between two of the windows in a highly-polished brass tub and then my mother would direct Patrick in the decorating of it. She would pick out of the box the blown-glass bubbles and the tiny birds and glimmering bells. Her small hands would put them with care into Patrick's huge hands and he would then attach them to the tree. Then there were the curled candles of red and blue and yellow wax in their gilt holders. I was allowed to watch this magical transformation, and sometimes even allowed to take into my cupped hands some of the less delicate of the glass decorations. The candles were never lit until Christmas Day, nor were the intriguing boxes and parcels heaped under the tree until after I had gone upstairs for my supper and bed, but the tall candle, that always glowed through the night, was placed in the window and I was allowed to light it the moment the tree was dressed. The curtains were then looped back so that the thin light could be seen from the garden after all the other lights in the house had been turned out.

I had awakened early, there was, in fact, only the barest glimmer of light in the sky outside my window. I got out of bed and put on my dressing-gown and, opening my bedroom door with great care, I went down the passage towards the large landing at the top of the stairs. This was lit from above by an ornate dome of glass, through which grey light was now creeping. There was no sound, except for that odd breathing that silence seems to make. I went down the stairs and across the hall and pushed open the drawing-room door.

Six pale rectangles and the straight flame of the candle made it possible for me to see the tall tree, the decorations glinting gently in the golden glow and beside the tree the shadowy figure of a child! Slowly she turned towards me as I stepped through the door. For a moment I felt as if my heart had stopped and then, as it thudded back to life again, I turned and ran out of the room, across the hall and up the stairs to the safety of my bed. I lay rigid under the bedclothes until I heard the early morning sounds of the maids moving around the house, and then, surprisingly, I fell asleep. After that I became more and more aware of her presence. If I were alone in the room I would suddenly become aware of her standing near me, her eyes always fixed on me in an unnerving blue stare. I would leave my book, or puzzle or merely my thoughts behind me and go out of the room. She never appeared while there were other people present, so little by little I began to avoid the drawing room when I was on my own. I even made excuses if my mother sent me to fetch something for her that she needed, as I knew that the child would be there, waiting.

When I was about fifteen I was sent to school in England. This was a painful time of my life; I neither appreciated the somewhat dreary disciplines inflicted on us, nor the boisterous friendliness of the other girls after so many years of solitude and freedom. My mind was open to learning however and I learnt what they offered me and in the course of learning forgot about my enemy. She did not forget about me, though, and as I went through the drawing-room door on my first day home from England, she rose from a chair by the fire and held out her hand towards me, as if she were the hostess and I the guest. Like myself she was no longer a child, but an attractive-looking girl with a long pale face and searching blue eyes. Without wanting to, I gave a small cry and my mother and her sister, who had paused for a moment in the hall, came into the room and the girl was gone.

My face must have been pale. My mother put her hand on my arm.

'You must be tired, my darling, after all that travelling. Come and sit down and tell us about all your adventures.'

She led me across the room to the chair where the girl had been sitting.

'No,' I said, with, I suppose, a certain shrillness in my voice. 'I'd rather not sit down at the moment.'

'Do what you wish.'

'I feel restless.'

'Overtired,' murmured my aunt. 'The child is overtired. She looks peaky. I'm sure they don't feed her properly in that establishment.'

'Of course they feed her properly,' said my mother, with irritation. 'You can't just pace up and down in here, child, like a caged lion. It makes me nervous.'

'I might just go up to my room for a while. Rest.'

'Anything you want, darling.'

'A little sleep,' my aunt suggested.

'Maybe.'

I left the room.

Upstairs, I lay on my bed and made a promise to myself never to go alone into the drawing room again.

Even so she continued to make her presence felt. Sometimes I would see, out of the corner of my eye, a slight movement, or hear the rustle of a skirt, feel a breath on the side of my face. Sometimes I was even aware of the shape her body had left in a chair in which she had been sitting waiting for me.

I became nervous and irritable. After a year or so, my parents, believing that my moodiness was due to some unhappiness at school, took me away and sent me to a small finishing school near Florence. There, I was happy for the first time, not just the uncaring happiness of childhood. I was filled with a real positive pleasure in being alive, in learning, in moving thoughtfully through the amazing world. I took like a duck to water to the countryside, the clear blue skies and the seamed brown faces of the peasants. I never missed the green rain-softened landscapes around Beauregard, the hedges of thorn and fuchsia, the long quiet evenings when the sun regretfully sighed its way down behind the low hills, leaving a band of gold lingering along the dark land, all those things in fact that make other emigrants sigh. I thrived in my new environment, and only became nervous when I returned home. I became filled with anxiety and my hands plagued me with their inability to rest. My mother would look at me with sad speculation in her eyes. I hated to make her unhappy, but I was unable to bring myself to explain to her or my father the cause of my unease and my very apparent desire to get away from Beauregard as quickly as possible. I think maybe they thought I was touched by some small element of madness and, indeed, maybe I have been all my life. They were gently indulgent towards me, but from time to time my mother became irritated by my behaviour. I would spend most of my time studying in my room, or else setting off for long, solitary walks along the narrow winding lanes and over the hills. Here I felt safe and almost happy, but each time I approached the house I could feel the tightening of the strings in my head, feel my hands becoming restless once more.

I had a small amount of money of my own at that time and, as the moment came for me to leave my school, I wrote to my parents asking them if I might stay in Florence to continue my studies in my own way. I had the grandiose idea in my mind that I would write over the years and have published a series of books on the various schools of Italian painting. I received an almost angry letter from my mother in reply. She reproached me with indifference towards my parents, with my unconcern for Beauregard, which would, after all, as she pointed out, be mine in the future, with her own approaching age and deep affection for me, and with the fact that I seemed to be unaware of what my duties in life might be, but she did not forbid me to stay in Florence, it was, she said, entirely up to me.

I found myself a room in a pensione and stayed. I enrolled myself at the university and studied hard. I felt free and very happy.

I made a brief visit to Ireland to see my parents. It was an unhappy experience for us all. The old weights descended on me again, the fear and constant agitation, the feeling that at any moment some unwanted thing would happen. Their obvious dissatisfaction with me made it all even worse. My father was growing old and needed grandsons, they explained to me. Good intelligent boys who knew about land and horses and loved the place, not the children of some impossible Italian who would care for nothing but lazing in the sun. A series of young men from all over the country were invited to dinner and picnics and tennis. I left so quickly that even my conscience pricked me, but not for long; the moment my train crossed the border between France and Italy I had forgotten my conscience once more. I was hard, I admit to this, but then, to live alone and as one wishes, one has to be hard.

Over the years I wrote my books and had them published. I became an expert. In Paris, New York and London, apart from Italy where I continued to live, my name became, in the world of art, one to conjure with. Everything went as I had planned.

After the death of my parents I sold Beauregard and

bought myself a charming villa on the slope of a hill overlooking my beloved Florence. As the years passed I moved from the field of mediaeval Italian painting to that of modern painting and I built up a fine small collection of the works of painters who are now modern no longer. Braque, Picasso, Matisse, Klee were amongst those whose paintings hang on my walls. I studied, I wrote, I travelled, I lectured. I immersed myself totally in my passion. I made many friends, but had neither time nor inclination to form deep and dependent relationships. In 1938 it became obvious what was going to happen in Europe, so with regret I sold my villa, packed my belongings and moved to New York, where I have lived ever since in great tranquillity. My books on mediaeval and Renaissance painting in Italy have become standard works. I have never had any worries, either financial or intellectual. I have never, until three days ago, returned to Ireland. I have succeeded in sliding over the surface of life with the same ease that a water-skier has as he planes across the seemingly calm surface of the sea.

Most of my closer acquaintances and colleagues have either died in the last few years or become cut off from life by illness. I have found myself that the increase of age and the diminution of respect from the young has made my life less pleasant than it was. I have never been a warm person, a person to whom others are instinctively drawn, irrespective of age or sex, and I have, over the past twenty years or so, found it difficult to change my fairly rigid views. I have become an oddity, a monument to a way of life and thought that no longer appeals to people.

I find the way in which people are choosing to lead their lives distasteful to me. I dislike the incompetence of modern thought, the fading values, the decay of faith. I feel I have no longer any reason for remaining alive.

It was shortly after I had come to this faintly depressing conclusion that thoughts of Beauregard began to creep back into my mind. To begin with, there were dreams; the garden, the smooth lawns, the trees drooping by the bay. The dreams came more and more frequently, evening sunshine sparkling on the granite walls, light moving on the window-panes, the smell of jasmine on the corner of the terrace. I wasn't upset in any way by the dreams, merely filled with nostalgia, something I despised in others. After a while they became daytime dreams. I would enter a room and for a moment I would be back in Beauregard, wrapped completely in the atmosphere of the past. Then the voice began in my head, gentle, courteous, insistent, calling me. There didn't seem to be any point in ignoring it. I knew what she wanted, the child who called. She wanted to give me back whatever it was she had taken so long ago.

I attended to those affairs that needed attending to, papers, settlements, arrangements in general, all tedious. All made more tedious by the fact that I wanted to be finished with them all, to be away.

I arrived at Shannon Airport two days ago. It was a beautiful blue day, and the sedate car that I had ordered was waiting for me, with an equally sedate driver, Mr Moriarty by name. He wears a flat black cap when driving me and only speaks when he is spoken to. I appreciate this. He is also a most unostentatious driver.

This hotel is at the opposite end of the village to Beauregard with the neat garden that I have written of sloping down towards the bay. The house, I seem to remember, used to belong to friends of my parents, and is now owned by a retired English couple who run it as an unexceptional, but pleasant hotel. The village street bends gently and then rushes precipitously down to a small harbour. The old stone houses lean companionably

together. The Protestant church sits on one of the small
hills at the back of the village, like an old lady, myself
perhaps, brooding over the great days of the past and,
opposite the wrought-iron gates, are the gates of Beauregard. I thought that to walk up the village street might
prove too tiring for me, so I arranged with Mr Moriarty
that he should drive me to the house yesterday afternoon
before tea. Someone must have removed the massive
gates for scrap and we turned in through the high pillars
and past the shell of the lodge. The avenue was rutted
and sadly overgrown but the tall chestnut trees were
elegant as they had always been. The front windows of
the house look out across the bay to the sea in the
distance. Because of the slope of the hill, the hall door is
level with the avenue in front and a narrow balcony runs
the whole way round the house, broadening at the back
to a terrace outside the drawing room, with steps that
lead down to what had once been a lawn. Brambles, ferns
and wild fuchsia now grow everywhere and there is a
smell of decaying masonry. I turned the handle of the hall
door and with a groan it moved. I felt a sudden distaste
for entering the dark hall and pulled the door towards me
once more. Mr Moriarty watched me with curiosity from
the car. I walked around the balcony until I came to the
first long window of the drawing room. To the right there
was a pattern of roofs and the squat tower of the church,
and the rooks were scattering in the sky above the trees
as they had always done. I turned towards the window.
The glass was thick with dust and salt blown from the sea
and I rubbed at it with my sleeve. The room seemed
larger than it had ever seemed and I could still see marks
on the walls where pictures had hung. Beside the fireplace
a tall woman was standing. She was handsomely dressed,
her thick grey hair looped back from her face in a chignon.
She smiled and held out her hand, in a gesture that I

remembered from the past. We stared at each other through the glass for a few minutes and then I turned away and went back to the car.

So, I shall go back. I will open the hall door and walk across the hall. The sun is shining and the drawing room will be filled with golden light. She will be there. She has waited a long time. She must be as tired as I am of the process of living. She will give and I will accept what she took from me so long ago and that will be the end.

I can hear the car on the gravel below. It is time to go. I am very happy.

JOHN McGAHERN

The Wine Breath

If I was to die, I'd miss most the mornings and the evenings, he thought, as he walked the narrow dirt-track by the lake in the late evening, and then wondered if his mind was failing, for how could anybody think anything as stupid: being a man he had no choice, he was doomed to die; and being dead he'd miss nothing, being nothing. And it went against everything in his life as a priest.

There was still the lake, the road, the evening, he tried to count, and he was going to call on Gillespie. Gillespie was sawing. Gillespie was always sawing. The roaring rise-and-fall of the two stroke stayed like a rent in the evening. And when he got to the black gate there was Gillespie, his overalled bulk framed in the short avenue of alders, and he was sawing not alders but beech, four or five tractorloads dumped in the front of the house. The priest put a hand to the black gate, bolted to the first of the alders, and was at once arrested by showery sunlight falling down the avenue. It lit up the one boot holding the length of beech in place, it lit the arms moving the blade slowly up and down as it tore through the beech, white chips milling out on the chain.

Suddenly, as he was about to rattle the gate loudly to see if it would penetrate the sawing, he felt himself (bathed as in a dream) in an incredible sweetness of light. It was the evening light on snow. The gate on which he had his hand vanished, the alders, Gillespie's formidable bulk, the roaring of the saw. He was in another day, the lost day of Michael Bruen's funeral nearly thirty years before. All was silent and still there. Slow feet crunched on the snow. Ahead, at the foot of the hill, the coffin rode slowly forward on shoulders, its brown varnish and metal trappings dull in the glittering snow, riding just below the long waste of snow eight or ten feet deep over the whole countryside. The long dark line of mourners following the coffin stretched away towards Oakport Wood in the pathway cut through the snow. High on Killeelan Hill the graveyard evergreens rose out of the snow. The graveyard wall was covered, the narrow path cut up the side of the hill stopping at the little gate deep in the snow. The coffin climbed with painful slowness, as if it might never reach the gate, often pausing for the bearers to be changed: and someone started to pray, the prayer travelling down the whole mile-long line of the mourners as they shuffled behind the coffin in the narrow tunnel cut in the snow.

It was the day in February 1947 that they buried Michael Bruen. Never before or since had he experienced the Mystery in such awesomeness. Now as he stood at the gate there was no awe or terror, only the coffin moving slowly towards the dark trees on the hill, the long line of the mourners, and everywhere the blinding white light, among the half-buried thorn bushes, and beyond Killeelan on the covered waste of Gloria Bog, on the sides of Slieve an Ierin.

He did not know how long he had stood in that lost day, in that white light, probably for no more than a moment. He could not have stood the intensity for any longer. When he woke out of it the grey light of the alders had reasserted itself. His hand was still on the bar of the gate. Gillespie was still sawing, bent over the saw-horse, his boot on the length of beechwood, completely enclosed in the roaring rise-and-fall of the saw. The priest felt as vulnerable as if he had suddenly woken out of sleep.

Shaken and somewhat ashamed to have been caught asleep in the actual day and life, without any protection of walls.

He was about to rattle the gate again, feeling a washed-out parody of something or other on what was after all nothing more than a child's errand: to tell the Gillespies that a bed had at long last been made available in the Regional Hospital for the operation on Mrs Gillespie's piles, when his eyes were caught again by the quality of the light. It was one of those late October days, small white clouds drifting about the sun, and the watery light was shining down the alder rows to fall on the white chips of the beechwood strewn all about Gillespie, some inches deep. It was the same white light as the light on snow. It was as simple as that. As he watched, the light went out on the beech chips, and it was the grey day again around Gillespie's sawing. It had been as simple as that. The suggestion of snow had been enough to plunge him in the lost day of Michael Bruen's funeral. Everything in that remembered day was so pure and perfect that he felt purged of all tiredness and bitterness, was, for a moment, eager to begin life again.

And, making sure that Gillespie hadn't noticed him at the gate, he turned back on the road. The bed wouldn't be ready for another week. The news could wait a day or more. Before leaving he stole a last look at the dull white ground about the saw-horse. The most difficult of things seem always to lie closest to us, to be always around our feet.

Ever since his mother's death he found himself stumbling into these dead days. Once crushed mint in the garden had given him back a day he'd spent with her at the sea in such reality that he had been frightened, as if he'd suddenly fallen through time; it was as if the world of the dead was as available to him as the world of the living. It was also humiliating for him to realize that she must have been the mainspring in his days. And now that the mainspring was broken the hands were weakly falling here and falling there. Today there had been the sudden light on the bits of white beech. He'd not have noticed it if he hadn't been alone, if Gillespie had not been so absorbed in his sawing. Before there must have been some such simple trigger that he'd been too ashamed or bewildered to notice.

Stealthily and quickly he went down the dirt-track by the lake till he got to the main road. To the left was the church in a rookery of old trees, and behind it the house where he lived. Safe on the wide main road he let his mind go back to the beech chips. They rested there around Gillespie's large bulk, and paler still was the line of mourners following the coffin through the snow, a picture you could believe or disbelieve but not be in. In idle exasperation he began to count the trees in the hedge along the road as he walked: ash, green oak, whitethorn, ash, the last leaves a vivid yellow on the wild cherry, empty October fields in dull wet light behind the hedges. This, then, was the actual day, the only day that mattered, the day from which our salvation had to be won or lost: it stood solidly and impenetrably there, denying the weak life of the person, with nothing of the eternal other than it would dully endure, while the day set alight in his mind by the light of the white beech, though it had been nothing more than a funeral he had attended during a dramatic snowfall when a boy, seemed bathed in the eternal, seemed everything we had been taught and told of the world of God.

Dissatisfied, and feeling as tired again as he'd been on his way to Gillespie's, he did not go through the church gate with its circle and cross, nor did he call to the sexton locking up under the bellrope. In order to be certain of being left alone he went by the circular path at the side round to the house, the high laurel hedge separating it from the graveyard and church. There he made coffee without turning on the light. Always when about to give birth or die cattle sought out a clean place in some corner of the field, away from the herd.

Michael Bruen had been a big kindly agreeable man, what was called a lovely man. His hair was a coarse grey. He wore loose-fitting tweeds with red cattleman's boots. When young he had been a policeman in Dublin. It was said he had either won or inherited money, and had come home to where he'd come from, to farm and to prosper.

He had a large family, and men were employed. All around, the yard and its big outhouses with red roofs rang with work: cans, machinery, raillery, the sliding of hooves, someone whistling; and in off the yard was the enormous cave of a kitchen, the long table down its centre, the fireplace at its end, the plates and pots and presses along the walls, sides of bacon wrapped in gauze hanging from hooks in the ceiling, the whole room full of the excitement and bustle of women.

Often as a boy the priest had gone to Michael Bruen's on some errand for his father. Once the beast was housed or the load emptied Michael would take him into the kitchen.

He remembered the last December evening well. He had driven over a white bullock. The huge fire of wood blazed all the brighter because of the frost.

'Give this man something,' Michael had led him. 'Something solid that'll warm the life back into him.'

'A cup of tea will do fine,' he had protested in the custom.

'Nonsense. Don't pay him the slightest attention. Empty bags can't stand.'

Eileen, the prettiest of Michael's daughters, laughed as

she took down the pan. Her arms were white to the elbows with a fine dusting of flour.

'He'll remember this was a good place to come to when he has to start thinking about a wife,' Michael's words gave licence to general hilarity.

It was hard to concentrate on Michael's question about his father, so delicious was the smell of frying. The mug of steaming tea was put by his side. The butter melted on the fresh bread on the plate. There were sausages, liver, bacon, a slice of black-pudding and sweetest grisceens.

'Now set to,' Michael laughed. 'We don't want any empty bags leaving Bruen's.'

Michael came with him to the gate when he left. 'Tell your father it's ages since we had a drink in the Royal. And that if he doesn't search me out in the Royal the next Fair Day I'll have to go over and bate the lugs off him.' As he shook his hands in the half-light of the yard lamp it was the last time he was to see him alive. Before the last flakes had stopped falling, and when old people were searching back to 'the great snows' when Count Plunkett was elected to find another such fall, Michael Bruen had died, and his life was already another such poor watermark of memory.

The snow lay eight feet deep on the roads, and dead cattle and sheep were found in drifts fifteen feet in the fields. All of the people who hadn't lost sheep or cattle were in extraordinary good humour, their own ill buried for a time as deep as their envy of any other's good fortune in the general difficulty of the snow. It took days to cut a way out to the main road, the snow having to be cut in blocks breast-high out of a face of frozen snow. A wild cheer went up as the men at last cut through to the gang digging in from the main road. Another cheer greeted the first van to come in, Doherty's bread van, and it had hardly died when the hearse came with the coffin of Michael Bruen. That night they cut the path up the side of Killeelan Hill and found the headstone beside the big yew just inside the gate and opened the grave. They hadn't finished digging when the first funeral bell came clearly over the snow the next day to tell them that the coffin had started on its way.

The priest hadn't thought of the day for years or of Michael Bruen till he had stumbled into it without warning by way of the sudden light on the beech chips. It did not augur well. There were days, especially of late, when he seemed to be lost in dead days, to see time present as a flimsy accumulating tissue over all the time that was lost. Sometimes he saw himself as an old man that boys were helping down to the shore, restraining the tension of their need to laugh as they pointed out a rock in the path he seemed about to stumble over, and then they had to lift their eyes and smile apologetically to the passers-by while he stood staring out to sea, having forgotten all about the rock in his path. 'It's this way we're going,' he felt the imaginary tug on his sleeve, and he was drawn again into the tortuous existence of the everyday, away from the eternal of the sea or the lost light on frozen snow across Killeelan Hill.

Never before, though, had he noticed anything like the beech chips. There was the joy of holding what had eluded him for so long, in its amazing simplicity: but mastered knowledge was soon no knowledge, unless it opened, became part of another, and what did the beech chips do but turn back to his own death?

Like the sudden snowfall and Michael Bruen's burial his life had been like any other, except to himself, and then only in odd visions of it, as a lost life. When it had been agreeable and equitable he had no vision of it at all.

The country childhood. His mother and father. The arrival at the shocking knowledge of birth and death. His attraction to the priesthood as a way of vanquishing death and avoiding birth. Oh, hurry it, he thought. There is not much to it. Many have it. There is not enough room. His father and mother were old when they married, and he was 'the fruit of old things', he heard derisively. His father had been a small farmer. His mother, a seamstress. He could still see the needle flashing in her strong hands, that single needle flash composed of thousands of hours.

'His mother had the vocation for him', perhaps she had, perhaps all the mothers of the country had, it had so passed into the speech of the country, in all the forms of both beatification and derision, and it was out of fear of death he became a priest, which becomes in its time the fear of life, and wasn't it natural to turn back to the mother in this fear: she was older than fear, having given death as well as life. There was then his father's death, the father accepting it as he had accepted all poor fortune all his life long, as his due, refusing to credit the good.

They had sold what they had together, and his mother had come to live with him, and was happy. She attended all the Masses and Devotions, took messages, and she sewed, though she had no longer any need, linen for the altar, soutanes and surplices, his shirts and all her own clothes. Sometimes her concern for him irritated him to exasperation but he hardly ever let it show. He had the outside duties of a priest. The fences on the past and future were secure. He must have been what is called happy, and there was a whole part of his life that without his knowing had come to turn to her for its own expression.

He discovered it when she began her death. He came home one summer evening to find all the lights in the house on. She was in the living room, in the usual chair. The table was piled high with dresses. Round the chair was a pile of rags. She did not look up when he entered, her still strong hands tearing apart a herring-bone skirt she had made only the year before.

'What on earth are you doing, Mother?' he caught her by the hands when she didn't answer.

'It's time you were up for Mass,' she said.

'What are you doing with all your dresses?'

'What dresses?'

'All the dresses you've just been tearing up.'

'I don't know anything about dresses,' and then he saw there was something wrong. She made no resistance when he led her up the stairs.

For some days she seemed absent and confused but, though he watched her carefully, she was otherwise very little difference from her old self, and she did not appear ill. Then he came home one evening to find her standing like a child in the middle of the room, surrounded by an enormous pile of rags. She had torn up every dress or article of clothing she had ever made. After his initial shock he did the usual and sent for the doctor.

'I'm afraid it's just the onset of senility,' the doctor said.

'It's irreversible?'

The doctor nodded. 'It very seldom takes such a violent form, but that's what it is. She'll have to be looked after.'

She recognized him when he visited the home during her first year there, but without excitement, as if he was already far away; and then the day came when he had to admit that she no longer knew who he was, had become like a dog kennelled out too long. He was with her when she died. She'd turned her face towards him. There came what seemed a light of recognition in the eyes, like a last glow of a match before it goes out, and then she died.

There was nothing left but his own life. There had been nothing but that all along, but it had been obscured, comfortably obscured.

He turned on the radio.

A man had lost both legs in an explosion. There was violence on the night-shift at Ford's. The pound had steadied towards the close but was still down on the day.

Letting his fingers linger on the knob he turned it off. The disembodied voice on the air was not unlike the lost day he'd stumbled into through the light on the beech chips, except it had nothing of its radiance – the funeral during the years he must have carried it around with him had lost the sheltered burden of the everyday, had become light as the air in all the clarity of light. It was all timeless, and seemed at least a promise of the eternal.

He went to draw the curtain. She had torn up all her clothes before she left the house. She had made the red curtain too with its pale lining but hadn't torn it. How often must she have watched the moonlight on the still headstones beyond the laurel, as it lay evenly on them this night. She had been afraid of ghosts. Old priests that had lived in this house, who through whiskey or some other ill had neglected to say some Mass for the dead – and because of the neglect the soul for whom the Mass should have been offered was forced to linger beyond its time in Purgatory – and the priest guilty of the omission could himself not be released until the living priest had said the Mass, and was forced to come at midnight to the house in all his bondage until that Mass was said.

'They must have been all good priests, Mother. Good steady old fellows like myself. They never come back,' he remembered his own idle reply as he drew the curtain, lingering as much over it as he had lingered over the turning off of the radio. He would be glad of a ghost tonight, be glad of any visitation from beyond the walls of sense.

He took up the battered and friendly missal, that had been with him all his adult life, to read the office of the day. On bad days he kept it till late, the familiar words that changed with the changing year, that he had grown to love, and were as well his daily duty. It must be surely the greatest grace of life, the greatest freedom, to have to do what we love because it is also our duty. Even here he wasn't able to read on this evening among the old familiar words for long. An annoyance came between him and the page, the Mass he had to repeat every day, the Mass in English. He wasn't sure whether he hated it or the guitar-playing priests more. It was humiliating to think that these had never been such a scourge when his mother had been alive. Was his life the calm vessel it had seemed, dully setting out and returning from the fishing grounds? Or had he been always what he seemed now? 'Oh yes. There you go again,' he heard the familiar voice in the empty room. 'Complaining about the Mass in the vernacular. When you prefer the common names of flowers to their proper names,' and the sharp, energetic, almost brutal laugh. It was Peter Joyce, he was not dead. Peter Joyce had risen to become a bishop at the other end of the country, to become an old friend that he no longer saw.

'But they are more beautiful. Dog rose, wild woodbine, buttercup, daisy . . .'

He heard his own protest. It was in an hotel that they used to go to every summer on the Atlantic, a small hotel where you could read after dinner without fear of a rising roar from the bar beginning to out-rival the Atlantic by ten o'clock.

'And, no doubt, the little rose of Scotland, sharp and sweet and breaks the heart,' he heard his friend quote maliciously. 'And it's not the point. The reason that names of flowers must be in Latin is that when flower lovers meet they know what they are talking about, no matter whether they're French or Greek or Arabs. They have a universal language.'

'I prefer the humble names, no matter what you say.'

'Of course you do. And it's parochial sentimentalists like yourself who prefer the *smooth sowthistle* to *Sonchus oleraceus* that's the whole cause of your late-lamented Mass in Latin disappearing. I have no sympathy with you. You people tire me.'

That had taken care of that annoyance, as its simple logic had once taken his breath away, but he was curiously tired after the vividness of the recall. It was only by a sheer act of will, sometimes having to count the words, that he was able to finish his office. 'I know one thing, Peter Joyce. I know that I know nothing,' he murmured when he finished. But when he looked at the room about him he could hardly believe it was so empty and dead and dry, the empty chair where she should be sewing, the oaken table with the scattered books, the clock on the mantel. And wildly and aridly he wanted to curse. But his desire to curse was as unfair as life. He had not wanted it.

And then, quietly, he saw that he had a ghost all right, that he had been walking around with for a long time, a ghost he had not wanted to recognize – his own death. He might as well get to know him well, he would never leave now. He was in the room, and had no mortal shape. Absence does not cast a shadow.

All there was was the white light of the lamp on the open book on the white marble; the brief sun of God on beech-wood, and the sudden light of that glistening snow, and the timeless mourners moving towards the yews on Killeelan Hill almost thirty years ago. It was as good as any, if there ever could be a good day to go.

And somewhere, outside this room that was an end, he knew that a young man not unlike what he had been once stood on a granite step and listened to the door bell ring, smiled as he heard a woman's footsteps come down the hallway, ran his fingers through his hair, and turned the bottle of white wine he held in his hands completely around as he prepared to enter a pleasant and uncomplicated evening, feeling himself immersed in time without end.

BRIAN MOORE

The Sight

Benedict Chipman never took a drink before five and never drank after midnight. He ate only a light lunch, avoided bread and potatoes and drank decaffeinated coffee. These self-regulations were, he sometimes thoughts, the only set rules he observed. Otherwise, he did as he liked.

Yet on the morning he returned to his eight-room apartment on Fifth Avenue after four days in hospital, his first act was to tell his housekeeper to bring some Scotch and ice into the library. When she brought it, he was standing by the window, looking out at Central Park. He did not turn around.

'Will that be all, sir?'

'Yes, thanks, Mrs Leahy.'

Chipman was fifty-two and a partner in a New York law firm. A few weeks ago, during his annual medical check-up, his doctor had noticed a large mole on his back and had recommended its removal. The operation was minor but, for Chipman who had never been in hospital before, the invasion of his bodily privacy by doctors, nurses and attendants had been humiliating and vaguely upsetting. Then, to complicate matters, while the biopsy showed the mole to be probably benign, the pathologist advised that 'to be completely sure', the surgeon should repeat the procedure but, this time, make a wider incision. The second biopsy had been scheduled for the end of the month. 'There's nothing to worry about,' the surgeon said. 'Just relax and come back ten days from now.'

But Chipman did not feel like relaxing. He felt nervous and irritable. As he poured the Scotch, he looked at the tray containing his mail. The first letter on the pile was postmarked Bishopsgate, NH. He had been born in Bishopsgate and for some reason he could not explain the sight of the postmark disturbed him. The letter was from his brother, Blake, who wrote that he and his wife were coming to New York to visit their son Buddy, a journalism major at Columbia. Buddy, it seemed, had learned that his uncle had been in hospital and Blake wrote that all three of them would like to call tomorrow afternoon. The letter irritated Chipman. He had no wish to see Blake and his family. He thought of his brother as a man who had never in his life owned a hundred dollars he didn't know about and whose relations with himself were sycophantic rather than fraternal, largely because of loans which Blake had not repaid.

At the library door, Mrs Leahy announced herself with a small prefatory cough. 'Mrs Kirwen is here, sir.'

'Show her in. And ask if she'd like something to drink.'

As he put his brother's letter down and rose to greet Geraldine, he heard her chatting with Mrs Leahy in the front hall.

'Is *he* having one? Oh, well then, a sherry, I think. By the way, how's your nephew, Mrs Leahy?'

'He still has the pleurisy, Ma'am. But he'll be all right.'

'Good, that's good news.

'Thank you, Mrs Kirwen.'

I never knew Mrs Leahy had a nephew, Chipman said to himself. But, come to think of it, he didn't know much about Mrs Leahy, although she had been with him for almost ten years. Lately, he had decided that his interest in other people was limited to the extent of their contributions to his purse, his pleasure or his self-esteem. He had a weakness for such aphoristic judgements. But, in this instance he also remembered another aphorist's warning: lack of interest in others is a first sign of age.

'Ben, darling, how are you? Shouldn't you have your feet up or something? You mustn't overdo it on your first day home.'

'Stop fussing.'

'I'm not fussing. Dr Wilking told me you should take it easy.'

'When was Wilking talking to *you*?'

'I met him in the corridor yesterday. Remember, he thinks I'm your wife.'

The surgeon, who did not know Chipman, had come in on them unexpectedly the night after the biopsy and found Geraldine, the buttons of her dress undone, lying on the hospital bed with Chipman. The surgeon had tactfully assumed she was Chipman's wife and had addressed her as such in the subsequent conversation. No one had contradicted him. 'That was a mistake,' Chipment said now, remembering. 'I should have said something.'

'Oh, what's it matter?'

'Well, my own doctor, Dr Loeb, knows I'm not married.'

'Oh, Ben. Who cares nowadays?'

At that point Mrs Leahy brought Geraldine's sherry. Geraldine, sipping it, put her long legs up on a yellow silk footstool. In this posture her skirt fell back, revealing her elegant thighs. Although impromptu erotic views normally pleased Chipman, this morning he was not pleased: he was irritated. 'Why can't you sit properly?'

'That's not a very nice thing to say when I've given up an important job to be with you today.'

'What job?'

'Remember, I tried out for the Phil Lewis show last week? Well, my agent called and said they want me for a second audition this afternoon. He says that usually means you've got the job. But, I'm not going.'

'Why not?'

'Because if I got the job it would mean I'd be on the coast for the next seven weeks. I'm not going to be three thousand miles away while you're in and out of hospital.'

'I'm not in and out of hospital. I'm just going back for a couple of days, that's all. Now, be a good girl. Phone and say you'll be glad to audition this afternoon.'

'No,' she said, suddenly looking as though she might begin to cry.

'But why not?'

'Because I've realized something, Ben. I'm in love with you. I don't want to be separated from you.'

In love with him? He remembered La Rochefoucauld's maxim that nothing is more natural or more mistaken than to suppose that we are loved. He knew Geraldine did not love him. She was an unsuccessful young actress, divorced from a television producer and in receipt of a reasonable alimony. His own role in her life was that of a suitable escort, an older man capable of providing presents and a good time, a friend who was good for a small loan and might not expect to see his money again. This sudden protestation of love was, he decided, no more than the familiar feminine need to justify having gone to bed with him. Geraldine would not give up her alimony: he did not want her to. The present arrangement suited him perfectly.

Nevertheless when she said that she loved him, for one moment he felt strangely elated. Then put his glass back on the silver tray and in its surface saw his face which seemed distorted, white, old. This foolishness must stop. 'Now, don't talk nonsense. Go and phone those people.'

'Are you trying to get rid of me?'

'Of course not. But if you go out to Hollywood this week it might work out very well. I was thinking of going to Puerto Rico. I thought I'd take a vacation. Lie in the sun until I have to go back into hospital.'

'Do you know people in Puerto Rico, is that it?'

'No. No. Look, Geraldine, you're *not* in love with me. My God, I'm twenty years older than you.'

'Age has nothing to do with being in love with someone.'

'Maybe not at your age. But at my age it has everything to do with it. Now go and make that phone call. Then I'll take you out and buy you lunch.'

She stood and picked up the otter coat he had helped pay for, trailing it behind her on the carpet as she moved across the room. At the door, she turned. 'So that's what you want. To go to Puerto Rico alone?'

'Yes.'

'Okay.'

She went into the hall. He listened to hear the tinkle as she picked up the phone, but instead heard the front door slam. He started across the room, thinking to go after her and bring her back, but stopped. He realized that he was close to the almost forgotten sensation of tears. Dammit, he'd just invented Puerto Rico to help her make up her mind about the audition. But now, as he felt himself tremble with anger – or was it weakness – he decided a short vacation in the sun might be the ideal way to wait out the next ten days. Maybe with Geraldine. He decided to suggest it at the office when he went in tomorrow.

There might be a little ill-feeling, though. He had already had a long vacation this summer. But what could they do? In the seventeen years he had been a member of the firm he had frequently demonstrated that his interests were not the law or the success of the partnership, but women, music, and his collection of paintings. However, on the day he joined the partnership he brought with him, as a wedding present from his father-in-law, an insurance company which dwarfed all other clients the firm did business with. And, although his marriage had subsequently broken up (his wife died eight years later in an alcoholic clinic, driven there, some said, by Chipman's behaviour with other women) his father-in-law had not held it against him. He still represented the insurance company and this power, coupled with his disregard for the firms's other clients, had driven his partners to revenge themselves on him in the only way they knew. They no longer invited him to their homes or, indeed, to any social function. Their boycott amused him: they bored him. They knew that he was amused and bored. Their dislike of him, he guessed, had long ago turned to hatred.

Yet on the following morning when he went to the office he was surprised to see George Geddes, the senior partner, come in at his doorway, eager, out of breath, and smiling like a job applicant. 'Ben, how are you, how're you feeling?'

'Hello, George.'

'So, how did it go?'

Directly behind Geddes, Chipman's secretary was at her desk in the outer office. He did not want her to hear what he had to say and so beckoned Geddes in and shut the door. 'Matter of fact, George, I wanted to have a word with you about that. Everything went very well, but they want me to go back, just as a precaution, and have a wider excision made. They've scheduled it for the 31st. I don't know. I'm feeling a little knocked out. I thought, if you don't mind, I might go and lie in the sun for a week. Not really come back to the office until next month.'

As he spoke he noticed that Geddes was already nodding agreement as though helping someone with a speech impediment. 'Of course, Ben, of course. No sense sitting around here. Good idea.'

'Well, thanks. Of course there are a few things I can clear up before I go.'

'No, no,' Geddes said. 'Let the juniors do some work for a change. Get on your feet again, that's the main thing.'

After Geddes had left. Chipman phoned a travel agency. He booked a double room with patio and pool in a first-class Puerto Rico resort hotel, starting the following Monday. He called in his juniors and reviewed their current handling of his clients' affairs. At noon he told his secretary that he was leaving and would not be back until the first week in December. Then he took a taxi to his apartment and for the second morning in a row broke his rule and made himself a drink.

But now his reason was celebratory. What a relief it had been to find Geddes agreeable for once. And there was a note saying Geraldine had telephoned. Obviously, her temper tantrum had not lasted. After pouring a Scotch he picked up the phone and dialled her number.

'Geraldine? Ben. First of all, I'm sorry about yesterday.'

'No, darling, it was my fault. Why shouldn't you go on a trip if you want to. When are you going, by the way?'

'No, tell me first, how was your audition?'

'I didn't go. It's a long story, I won't bore you with it.'

'Does that mean you might be free to join me in Puerto Rico?'

'Ben, do you mean it?'

'Of course. I booked a double with patio and pool in the Caribe Imperial. Or would you rather I got you a room of your own?'

'No, no.'

'Good. And what about the weekend? Are you free?'

'Do you mean now? Yes. Completely.'

'Well, so am I. Or, almost. I have to be here tomorrow afternoon when my brother and his family are coming. But that shouldn't take more than an hour.'

'Are we thinking of the same thing?'

'I hope so.'

'All right, darling. Come on down. I'll be waiting.'

'I'll be right there.'

His brother's hand, tentative at first, went out to finger the Steinway's polished surface, then boldly stroked the wood. His brother's head turned, afternoon sunlight merciless on the thin grey hair, the pink skull-cap of skin beneath. His brother smiled, ingratiatingly and falsely intimate. 'Beautiful piano, eh, Ben?' his brother said. 'You must play something for us before we go. I mean, if you feel up to it.'

'Oh yes, Ben, you must,' said his brother's wife who, he knew, did not care at all for music.

If he felt up to it. What would they say if they knew he had come up from the village two hours ago after a night of screwing that would exhaust anyone? Perhaps it would not exhaust Blake's wife, though. One summer, when their son Buddy was still a brat in rompers, Chipman had gone to visit them at their summer cottage on Cape Cod. He was sunbathing in the dunes when Blake's wife came up from the beach, drying her hair on a towel, her shoulderstraps undone, her swimsuit set from the sea. She did not see him until she stumbled on him and when he reached up and pulled her down, she did not say a word. Later they walked hand in hand over the dunes towards the cottage. Blake was sitting on a deck chair on the lawn, reading a book and the child was on the porch playing with an old inner tube. Man and child looked up and his brother's wife at once let go of his hand and ran to kiss her child. She avoided Chipman for the rest of that evening and the following morning he thought it wise to pretend a business engagement in Boston. He had not been to stay with them since.

'Let Buddy play something,' he said, knowing that Buddy's atrocious playing would please them much more than his own. And so Buddy obediently flopped down on the piano bench, looked disdainfully at the music scores in front of him, then poised his large hands over the keys. 'What'll it be, Uncle Ben?'

'You choose,' Chipman said. Years ago, prodded by Blake's wistful hints about the child's musical inclinations, he had paid for a series of piano lessons for Buddy. The money had been wasted for Buddy's musical talents were a myth, the first of a long series of efforts on his parents' part to make Chipman feel a special affection for the boy. All had failed. Buddy's only effect on his uncle was to relieve him of any regrets about not having had a son of his own.

But now he pretended to listen as Buddy stumbled through some Cole Porter tunes, noticing as he mimed attention that Buddy's parents seemed nervous as though they had quarrelled before coming and were now trying to cover it up by a surfeit of polite remarks to each other. Chipman was uninterested. He simple wanted them to go and so, when Blake glanced at last in his direction, he pretended drowsiness. It worked. As his son thumped to a pause in the music, Blake stood up. 'Thanks, Bud, but we'd better not overtire your uncle. Besides your mother and I want to catch that Wyeth show at the Met before our train leaves.'

Then he turned to Chipman. 'Ben, could I have a word with you?'

As on signal both Buddy and his mother left the room. It was, Chipman knew, the usual prelude to Blake's asking for money, but today a loan seemed well worth it to get rid of them. He went to his desk, aware the Blake, if left to his devices, would take at least five minutes to come to the point. He opened a drawer and took out his chequebook.

'What's that for?' Blake asked sharply.

'Nothing.'

'Put that away, will you,' Blake said. 'I'm ashamed that I owe you so much. As a matter of fact, Ben, it wasn't that at all. It was just that we wondered if you'd like to come up to Bishopsgate to convalesce until you go back into the hospital.'

'Thanks, but I'm going to Puerto Rico.'

'Oh. Puerto Rico?'

'Yes, I thought I'd like to lie in the sun for a few days.'

'Oh, that's a pity, we were looking forward to the thought of having you. You and I haven't spent much time together these last years.'

'I know. Well, maybe some other time.'

'Any time,' Blake said. 'I'd like us to go for walks around the old place and have talks and all that. I'd like that a lot.'

And then, abruptly, Blake took hold of his hand and squeezed it. 'I'd really like it, Ben.'

'Well, we'll do it,' Chipman said, uneasily, beginning to move towards the hallway where the others waited. As they came out he saw Blake's wife glance at her husband and saw Blake give a small, almost imperceptible shake of his head. Buddy came forward, hand out, smiling. 'Goodbye, sir.'

'Goodbye,' Chipman said. 'Goodbye, Blake.'

His sister-in-law came towards him. He held out his hand. She ignored it and raced up to kiss him on the cheek. He was astonished. 'Goodbye,' his sister-in-law said. 'Take care of yourself.'

The elevator came. They went down.

Confused, Chipman closed the door of his apartment. It was as though he had found an interesting passage in a dull book and had seen it snatched away before he had time to finish it. Why had Blake's wife kissed him, she who had so carefully avoided kissing him ever since that summer on the beach? And why had Blake come up with this unprecedented invitation to visit them at Bishops-gate? Why were they being so kind all of a sudden? Come to think of it, everyone had been abnormally kind these past two days – Geraldine, Geddes, Blake. It was irritat-ing, dammit, to be treated as though, all of a sudden, he were made of glass. How did La Rochefoucauld put it? *Pride does not wish to owe: nor vanity to pay.* He didn't want favours from anyone. So, why did they try?

He had reached the library door before the thought and the answer came to him. He was going to die. That was why they were all being so gentle. They knew something he didn't know. A wider excision, that was what the surgeon said. 'To be completely sure,' the pathologist said. They hadn't told him the truth, that was it. 'Just relax,' the surgeon said.

He must not panic. He must call Dr Loeb, his internist and put the question to him quite casually, implying that he already knew all about it. He must go to the phone now and clear things up.

He went into his bedroom and closed the door so that Mrs Leahy would not overhear him. He phoned Dr Loeb but the answering service said Dr Loeb was out of town for the weekend and a Dr Slattery was taking his calls. So that was no use. The surgeon's name was Wilking. He looked up the number. The answering service said Dr Wilking wasn't in, but would he leave a message. He left his name and number and lay down on the bed, worrying. After five minutes he telephoned again and said it was an emergency. He must reach Dr Wilking at once. This time, the answering service gave him a number to call. Dr Wilking answered.

'Dr Wilking, this is Benedict Chipman speaking. Now, I know this may sound silly to you, but was there anything about that operation of mine that I should know about?'

'Why do you ask, Mr Chipman?'

'I just want to know the truth. It's important, doctor.'

'Well, look, Mr Chipman, it's pretty much as I told you. I don't think you have anything to worry about.'

'Is that the truth? I want the truth.'

'Yes, what can I say? Look, Mr Chipman. The best thing you can do now is relax. Your wife mentioned you might go off for a short vacation. I think that's a good idea.'

'How the hell can I take it easy? For God's sake, doctor, that's like telling a man to take it easy in the condemned cell while you decide whether or not he's to be reprieved.'

'Oh, come on now, Mr Chipman. I wouldn't say that.'

'Of course, you wouldn't,' Chipman shouted. 'And that girl isn't my wife, do you hear? So anything you have to say, just say it to me!'

He put the receiver down without waiting to hear the surgeon's reply. He looked at his bed. This was the bed he might die in. He turned from it and went into his library. Small picture lights lit his collection of Krieghoff landscapes. When he died these pictures would be sent to the Bishopsgate Art Gallery to be exhibited in a special room with a brass plaque over the door, identifying him as their donor. They would arrive after his body, which would be buried under a plain headstone in the episcopal cemetery, next to his parents' grave. How many people

ever read donors' plaques or the names on headstones? A
year from now he would be forgotten.

But wasn't that jumping the gun, giving in to a bad case
of jitters unsupported by any evidence? How could they
know he was going to die when they hadn't even done the
second biopsy yet? What were they keeping from him?
Whatever it was had frighened Geraldine into suddenly
declaring her love. But she doesn't love me, Chipman
decided, she pities me. Pity is what everyone feels for me
now; Geraldine, Geddes, Blake, Blake's wife. Yet how
could they all know this thing about me? Geraldine has
never met Geddes. Or Buddy. Who told Buddy, for
instance?

Chipman went to his desk, searching it and then went
to the telephone table in the hall. He knew he had a
number for Buddy someplace, and when he found it and
dialled it, it was a fraternity house. No one answered for
a long time and then some boy told him Buddy wasn't in,
and that he didn't know when he would be back. As
Chipman replaced the receiver, Mrs Leahy passed him in
the hall, going down the corridor to her own room. Only
one person might have spoken to Buddy, to Geddes, to
Geraldine. One person who would answer the phone
when people called here to ask how he was. He went
down the corridor to the far end of the apartment and
stopped outside Mrs Leahy's door. He almost never came
into this part of the apartment, near the pantry and wine
cellar, and past the kitchen. He stood for a moment and
then, without knocking, he opened the door.

He had not seen the inside of Mrs Leahy's room for
years. Sometimes he heard the television sound, turned
low, and sometimes she would leave the door open, at
night, when she went to answer the phone. Now, his eyes
went from the television set to the horrid rose and green
curtains, the cheap coloured lithograph of some saint, to

the crucifix, entwined with fading palm which hung over
what seemed to be a sewing table. It was the sort of room
he used to glimpse through upper-storey windows, years
ago, when he still rode the subways, a room which
screamed a sudden mockery of all other rooms in his
elegant apartment. And its occupant, her back to him,
unaware of his presence, was the perfect figure in this
interior. In her pudgy fingers, the surprise of a cigarette:
on her lap, inevitably, the garish headlines of the *Daily
News*.

'Mrs Leahy?'

She turned. Her grey head was that of a stranger,'s
utterly changed by the absence of her uniform cap. 'Oh,
did you ring, sir? Is the bell not working?'

'No, I didn't ring.'

'Can I get you something, sir? Are you all right?'

By this time she had stubbed her cigarette and had
pinned on the familiar housemaid's cap. 'A little whisky?'
she said. 'Or, are you hungry, sir? Would you like a
sandwich?'

'Whisky,' he said. 'And I want to talk to you.'

'Yes, Mr Chipman.' Swiftly she moved past him going
down the corridor to the monastic neatness of her kitchen.
She did not, of course, expect him to follow her into the
kitchen and looked up, surprised, when he did.

'A little water with it, sir? I'll bring it into the library,
will I?'

'No. Sit down, Mrs Leahy. Please.'

As she placed the bottle of Scotch, ice and a glass and
pitcher of water on a tray, he drew out one of the chrome
and leather kitchen chairs, indicating that she should sit
in at the table. As she did, he saws a red rash of
embarrassment rise from her neck to her cheeks. They
had never been informal together. He sat opposite her
and poured himself a Scotch. 'Now,' he said. 'Let me ask

you something. Are you the person who's been telling
people I have cancer?'

'Me, sir?'

'Yes, you.'

She did not answer him at once. She put her veiny old
hands on the table, joined them as in an attitude of
prayer, then looked at him with the calculating, ready-to-
bolt caution of a rodent. He had never before noticed this
animal quality of hers. Why, she's a hedgehog, he
decided. She's Mrs Tiggy Winkle.

'Yes, sir. It was me.'

He must keep calm. He must not let her know that he
was ignorant of all the facts of his illness. 'I see. And who
told *you* that I might have cancer?'

'Mrs Kirwen, sir.'

'And what did she say, exactly?'

'Ah, she didn't say you had cancer, she said they were
going to operate on you again just to be sure. There was
always the chance, she said. And I said to her I thought I
should let Mr Buddy know. On account of your brother,
sir. And then Mr Geddes rang up about you. And I told
him. To let him know, like.'

'Oh, you did, did you? Well, I like the way you let
them know. They think I'm going to die. I could see it on
my brother's face this afternoon. He thinks I'm going to
die.'

'I'm very sorry, now, Mr Chipman.'

'Mrs Kirwen *didn't* say to you I had cancer, did she?
She didn't say the doctors had told her something they
hadn't told me. Or, did she?'

'Ah, no, sir, Mrs Kirwen never said you were going to
die. 'Tis not Mrs Kirwen's fault at all. 'Tis my fault, and
I'm very sorry now.'

'Tell me, Mrs Leahy. Do you dislike me?'

'Oh, no, sir.'

'Then why did you tell those people that I'm going to die?'

'Ah, well, sir, that's a long story. And I'm very sorry to be bringing you news like that. But them doctors don't know everything, now do they?'

'What do you mean?' He was shouting, but he could not stop himself. 'Just exactly what the hell do you mean, Mrs Leahy?'

Mrs Leahy, avoiding his eye, stared down to her joined hands. 'Well, sir, you see, I have something now, something not many people have. And there's times I wish I didn't let me tell you.'

'Didn't what? Didn't have what?'

'I have the sight, sir. The second sight.'

'Second sight?' Chipman repeated the words with the joy of a man repeating the punch line of a joke. 'Well. And there I was . . .' Beginning to shake with amusement, he lifted his glass and drank a great swallow of whisky. 'You mean you dreamed it, or something like that?'

'Yes, sir. Last Monday, the night before your operation.'

'Now let me get this straight,' Chipman said. 'Mrs Kirwen told you nothing except what you've told me. The truth is nobody *knows* I have cancer. There's absolutely no proof of it at all.'

'That's right, sir.'

'My God, do you realize the mischief you've caused?'

'I'm very sorry, now. I see I shouldn't have said anything. I beg your pardon, sir.'

'It was a disgraceful thing to do!

'Yes, sir. I'm sorry, sir. Maybe I should give you my notice?'

'No, no,' Chipman poured himself a second drink.

Suddenly, he felt like laughing again. 'Well, now,' he said. Unconsciously, and for the first time in their acquaintance, he found himself slipping into an imitation of her Irish brogue. 'And how long have you, had this "sight"?'

'Ah, a long time, now. I noticed it first when I was only fourteen.'

'You dream about things and then they happen, is that it?'

'In a way, sir.'

'What do you mean? Tell me.'

'I'd rather not, now, sir. I'm sorry about speaking to those people. I only meant it for your sake, sir.'

'Now, wait. I'm just interested in this premonition of yours. Now, what happened in my case? You had a dream?'

'Yes, just the dream, sir. Nothing else.'

'What do you mean, nothing else?'

'Well you see, first there's the dream. And then, later on, you see, there's a second sign.'

'And what's this second sign?'

'It's a look I do see on the person's face.'

'A look?'

'Yes. When the trouble is very close.'

Chipman, in the act of downing his second Scotch, looked at her over the rim of his glass. Ignorant, stupid old creature with her hedgehog eyes and butterfat brogue. Some primitive folk nonsense, typically Irish, he supposed; it was their religion that encouraged these fairy tales. 'When it's close,' he said. 'What does that mean?'

'When it's close to the time, sir.'

'So, I take it you haven't seen this look on my face. Not yet.'

'That's right, sir.'

'When do you think you'll see it?'

'I don't know that, sir. Better not be asking me things like that. It's no pleasure to me to be seeing the things I do see. That's the God's own truth, sir.'

'But how do you know you'll see it? Do you always see if after you have this dream?'

'I'd say so, sir.'

'Give me an example.'

'Well, I saw it on my own sister, sir, the night before she died. I had a dream and saw her in the dream, and when I woke up she was sleeping in the bed with me and I lit the lamp and looked at her face. I saw it in her face. And the very next night she was killed by a bus on her way home. I was fourteen at the time.'

'Tell me about another time.'

'Ah, now, what's the use, sir.'

'No, you started this, Mrs Leahy. I want to hear more.'

'And I don't want to tell you, sir.'

'But you told Mrs Kirwen and Mr Geddes and my nephew. You weren't afraid to tell them this fairy tale.'

'Ah, I didn't tell them that at all, sir. Sure they wouldn't believe it. I just said I had information, I couldn't say more. But that the doctors were very worried about you.'

'*Did* you?' Again, he felt furious at her. 'How dare you, Mrs Leahy!'

'I'm sorry, sir. I wanted to be a help to you, sir. I mean I wanted Mrs Kirwen and your family and all, to be good to you now in your time of trouble.'

I must *not* lose my temper with a servant, Chipman told himself. 'All right,' he said. 'You told me about your sister. Give me another example.'

'My husband, sir, God rest his soul. I dreamed about him June 2nd, 1946, and he was took on the 2nd November, the same year. And on the 1st November I saw the look on his face. I begged him not to go to work the next day, but he didn't heed me. He fell off a scaffolding. He never lived to see a priest.'

'Wait,' Chipman said. 'Both these deaths were from accidents, not illnesses.'

'Yes, sir.'

'Well, have you had any premonitions about deaths from illness?'

'Well, Jimmy, one of the doormen in this building. I saw him in a dream four months before he died of heart disease. And on the day he was taken I went to see him in the hospital. And I saw the look on him.'

'Indeed.' Slowly, Chipman finished his Scotch.

'Of course, 'tis not always departures. Deaths. Sometimes I do see arrivals. Do you remember, sir, the night you came home from Washington, last New Years Eve it was. I had your dinner waiting for you. I dreamed the night before that you would come at nine, wanting your dinner. And you did.'

As a matter of fact, Chipman thought, I remember it well. I remember thinking she'd prepared that roast lamb for herself and some crony. Extrasensory perception, premonition: of course all that was only one jump away from teacup reading, table turning, spiritualistic quacks. But she dreamed of my death.

'So, Mrs Leahy. You dreamed of me, again, the other night. But this time it wasn't about my arrival?'

She nodded.

'Tell me the dream.'

'Ah, don't be asking, sir.'

'But I am asking. If you go around telling false stories to people about my death, you have the obligation to tell me the truth about what prompted you to do it. Now, what did you see in this dream?'

'I saw the shroud sir. You came in the room and you were wearing the shroud.'

'A shroud. That means death.'

'Yes, sir.'

'When?'

'Ah, now, I don't know that, sir.'

'But you will know, as soon as you see this look on my face, is that it?'

'Yes, sir. I'd know the time, then.'

'I see,' Chipman said. 'And now I suppose you'd like me to cross your palm with silver, so that you'll tell me when I must make my funeral arrangements. Well, Mrs Leahy, I'm going to disappoint you. A few minutes ago, when I thought of the mischief you've done and the worry you've caused my family and friends, I was quite prepared to let you go. But, believe me, I wouldn't let you go now for all the gold in Fort Knox. A year from now, Mrs Leahy, you and I will sit here together. We'll have a drink together, this time, this date, one year from now.'

'God willing and we will, sir.'

He stood up, suddenly feeling his drink, his chair making a screeching noise on the linoleum floor. 'And now,' he said, 'I'd better phone Mrs Kirwen and those other people and explain what's really happened.'

'Yes, sir. I'm very sorry.'

He went back into the library. There was no point in being angry with her, it was a joke really. He should be celebrating. The doctors weren't alarmed, and even if they found some malignancy, there are all sorts of treatments, cobalt bombs, chemotherapy and so on. To think that stupid old hedgehog had set all this in motion – Geddes, Buddy, even Geraldine. Poor Geraldine.

He went to his shelves, took down a volume of the *Encyclopaedia Britannica* and read the entry under cancer. He then read the entry under clairvoyance. When he had finished, he replaced the books and rang the bell.

'Yes, sir.'

She stood at the door, her uniform cap on straight, the perfect housekeeper, a treasure, his women friends said. 'I'd like some ice and water,' he said.

She nodded and smiled. Mrs Tiggy Winkle. When she came back with the tray, he tried to affect a bantering tone. 'Now, just in theory, mind you, just for curiosity's sake. When do you think you'll see that look on my face?'

'I don't know, sir. I hope it will be a long, long time off. Was there anything else, sir?'

'No.'

'Goodnight, sir.'

She bobbed her head in her usual half curtsey of withdrawal. When she had gone he made himself a fresh drink, then went to the window and stood looking down at Fifth Avenue. People in evening dress were getting out of rental Cadillac limousines in front of his building, laughing and joking, going to some function.

An hour later, he was still standing there. The room behind him was quite dark. He heard no sound in the apartment. He walked into the lighted hallway and went towards the kitchen. She was not there. He went past the kitchen, going towards her room. He stood in front of her door, trembling with excitement. He knocked.

'Yes, sir.'

She was sitting in her armchair, stitching the hem of an apron. The television set had been turned off.

'You were waiting for me, weren't you?'

'No, sir. Would you be wanting dinner, sir?'

'You should know I don't want dinner. I thought knowing things like that was one of your specialities.'

She bent to her sewing.

'Mrs Leahy, I want to ask you something. What if I fired you tonight? You'd never see the look would you?'

'I suppose not, sir.'

'Then you'd never know if you'd been right. I mean

supposing you never saw my death in the paper. You wouldn't know, would you?'

She bit the edge of her thread.

'Well, answer me.'

'Yes, sir, I'd know.'

'Look at me!' Even to himself, his voice sounded strange. 'You haven't looked at me since I came into the room.'

She folded the apron, placed it on the sewing table and turned around. He went towards her, his face drained. As her eyes met his, he thought again of an animal. As animal does not think: it knows or it does not know. He sat on the edge of a worn sofa, facing her.

'Well?' His voice was hoarse.

'Well what, sir?'

'You know what. Am I still all right?'

'Yes, sir.'

'Mrs Leahy,' he said. 'You wouldn't lie to me, would you? I mean you'd tell me if you saw it.'

'I suppose so, sir. I might be afraid to worry you, though.'

His hands gripped hers. 'No, no, I want to know. You must tell me. Promise me you'll tell me when the time comes?'

Tears, the unfamiliar tears of dependence, blurred his vision: made the room tremble. Gently, she nodded her head.

PETER SOMERVILLE-LARGE

Rich and Strange

Jack Colley's eldest child had known our daughter in playgroup years, then at school. They had been in and out of each other's houses, tongues orange from ice lollies, sharing roller skates, bicycles and felt pens. Deirdre came to our house more than Rachel went to hers; in winter we ran our central heating regularly and our place never smelt of nappies. They played upstairs or in the garden as weather dictates; they slumped over the same homework and skimped it to watch the children's programmes. Deirdre's cheeks bulged a little into her jaw like a bloodhound or a pear. Her flaxen hair was beginning to have dark streaks, and would end up mousy or dark brown. She had round eyes like one of her dolls, making her look surprised.

From time to time she brought over her sleeping-bag to spend the night, usually, it seemed, when she was about to acquire another sibling. On those occasions Jack and his aptly-named Breda distributed their children among friends and relatives for the duration of Breda's stay at the Rotunda.

Relationships with the parents of children's friends have an element of gradual coercion. Our acquaintance with the Colleys progressed from shared school runs to female coffee mornings to formal entertainment to an exchange of small Christmas presents. In roughly the same time that the Black Death took to cross Asia and Europe, we found ourselves friends. Jack wasn't a bad fellow. He worked in local government, where his job, though not all that well paid, was inflation-proof and promised an adequate pension. The boys had their names down for Gonzaga. He ran a big car, while Breda drove an ancient Morris Minor. Morris Minors have acquired a disreputable image, and tend to be driven by mountainy men or delinquent teenagers; but the Colley's was grey and clean with a respectability that belonged to a previous decade. Both cars, like ours, were insured with the Private Motorists Protection Association. We didn't have all that much more in common.

For several summers running we took our holidays in rotation, since we lived in the same neighbourhood. In this way we could watch each other's houses and feed the other family's cat. The Colleys used to go abroad to some place like Benidorm or Lido di Jesolo, leaving behind a baby or two with Breda's mother. Then came the year when, like a lot of other people, they were kept at home by the falling pound. Jack bought a second-hand Sprite caravan and planned to take the whole family to Kerry. Breda's people came from there, and she had memories of holidays on relatives' farms.

Our holiday occurred first. We were back at the end of July, and a week later the Colleys made their ponderous departure, starting early in the morning. We waved from the bedroom as the Sprite passed, rattling over the concrete on its way towards the Limerick road.

That summer was exceptionally hot. In our suburb the long spell of glittering weather became a time to be endured. During August I escaped the office fairly often, and we drove to beaches south of the city. The Colleys sent us a postcard from Dingle with a picture of two currachs. But there were other things to think about besides the Colleys and after they returned we didn't see them until school began. The first days of September ended the hot weather abruptly so that the children went back in rain. On the Friday of the second week of September when I came home from work I found a sleeping-bag in the hall.

'Deirdre's staying,' Anne told me.

'What's wrong?'

'Breda's not well.'

'Miscarriage?'

Anne's voice took on the hush of scandal.

'A bit of a breakdown. Dr Byrne's sending her to the psychiatric unit at Elm Park. I feel terrible not having once seen them since they got back . . .'

'Will we be stuck with Deirdre for weeks?'

'Not at all. Only a couple of days. Breda's mother is coming up to take charge.'

'Poor old Jack. I'll give him a ring later on.' These things have become less embarrassing. In our suburb psychiatric troubles are more common than adultery.

'You won't get anything out of him.'

'I didn't mean that. I just feel sorry for the poor bastard.'

'All he would say when I asked him was that she was under a bit of stress.'

'Anyone who takes five children off in a caravan is looking for stress.'

In the end I left Jack and his troubles to himself. Over tea I noticed that the children were all in bad form. There was none of the usual giggling among the girls, no nudging or back-chat or teasing Tommy. In fact, hardly any conversation at all. I knew that Anne wanted to dump Deirdre about her mother, but there was something formidable about the child's reserve. I tried to ease things up with a few knock knock jokes and questions about school, and Miss Synott's boy friend, a subject that usually promoted ribald laughter. Not a stir from either of them. Deirdre turned down her eyes like a propositioned nun.

Anne laid out her sleeping-bag as usual on our safari bed which was set up in Rachel's room. The girls didn't play or talk late. After midnight Deirdre woke us with screams. She couldn't remember, she said, when I asked, what the bad dream had been about.

Ten minutes after we had all settled down I found Rachel standing beside my bed.

'Go back to your room at once.'

'She's at it again.' We listened. We could hear her across the passage, not so loud, more like groans.

'The same silly word,' Rachel said.

As usual Anne had closed her eyes again with a determinedly sleepy grunt. I have always been the one to get up and cope with the children. I put on my dressing-gown again and walked over into Rachel's room, half-lit by the light on the landing. Deirdre thrashed about in her sleeping-bag, muttering.

'Misericordia, miscericordia . . .'

'That's what she was saying before.'

Her face was covered with perspiration. I debated whether to wake her, when she solved the problem by waking herself.

'Another dream?' She nodded and put her thumb in her mouth. I went down to the kitchen to fetch a couple of mugs of hot milk, knowing that Rachel would insist on having one too. When I got back upstairs, both of them were lying quite silently in their respective beds. As I gave Deirdre two Junior Aspirin, I asked her. 'What's all this about misericordia? Is it a word that you hear in church?' Her upper lip, its line emphasized by a white moustache of milk, drew back like an angry cat. Her round eyes didn't have a look of surprise, but of terror.

'Never mind . . .' Rules were suspended, and I read aloud a soothing passage from *A Bear Named Paddington*.

Then we went back to sleep. I remembered that Mass has been said in English for the past decade or so.

Next morning the girls seemed fine, as is so often the case after a wicked night, while Tommy had slept through it all. Anne wanted to drive to Superquinn for Saturday's big shopping. In the usual way we would have all gone together so that I could help with the bags of groceries and the children could spend their pocket money. But the rain was pouring down, and after all the excitements Anne and I both felt that it might be better if the children and I stayed at home and she managed on her own. The girls seemed indifferent while Tommy was persuaded with a promise of extra sweets. None of them really wanted to go out in the wet.

After I had washed the breakfast things I settled down in the kitchen with the paper. When the yells came from the playroom I only felt annoyance. They were of a type instantly recognizable, the unmistakable sounds of resentful children in unison making a noise like angry sheep.

'What's going on up there?' Rachel seemed to be siding with her brother, something I had hardly known her to do since the time Tommy began to speak. In the end I went storming upstairs.

Tommy keeps his Action Man meticulously, far better than Rachel maintains her dolls. His model has a beard, a fair pelt moulded to his rubbery little face. His wardrobe includes the uniforms of a Commando, a tank commander, a Red Devil and a storm-trooper, while he possessed accessories like a rifle rack, a mortar and a belt-feed machine-gun.

He was not dressed in his Commando clothes that Saturday, or in any of his other outfits. He wore a long shirt, borrowed from a teddy bear.

He had been hanged.

It gave me quite a shock to see him. The gallows, made

out of Lego, was on two legs with a bar across like a football goal without the net. His hands were tied behind him with knitting wool and the noose was also made out of wool which had been strengthened by being plaited. Rachel and Tommy stood crying, but they didn't touch him. They let him hang, his plastic toes a couple of inches above the cork tiles of the playroom floor. Deirdre looked on serenely.

She didn't object when I cut the Action Man down with nail scissors. Tommy stopped crying, to test his soundbox by pulling a string and listening to him give orders in an American accent, telling his men to go over the top or something similar. Thankfully Anne came back soon after to sort things out. After lunch the rain was still coming down, so they chose to look at television. But that also ended in a row.

'What was it this time?'

Anne said, 'They wouldn't agree on what to watch. Deirdre is becoming impossible. She wouldn't look at the film on RTE and she and Rachel were struggling with the knobs – they almost had the set over. There's only racing or wrestling on the English channels.'

'What was it about? Something horrific? She seems in such a funny state.'

'It was only an old pirate film. Stewart Granger. Deirdre's seen far more grisly things in her time. Remember when we all went to *Jaws*?'

The children continued to bicker so that several times Rachel came to Anne and tried to win her sympathy with a whining tale. Then the television improved, and they sat down silently watching it. I gave Jack a ring, but there was no reply; we concluded that he must have gone down to Naas to fetch his mother-in-law. Anne rang round her friends to find out what their opinion was about giving Deirdre a spot of Valium. I don't know what the verdict was, but the night passed more or less undisturbed. Although the child called out several times, she didn't wake the others, and was deeply asleep the couple of times I went across to her.

When I took her home on Sunday morning Breda's mother was there to greet us. In the kitchen there was a smell of roasting meat, and three of the younger children were seated on the window-seat in front of a table littered with crisp bags, blue tack, Playdough, paper and felt pens. After giving her grandmother a kiss Deirdre went straight upstairs to the chilly bedrooms above. I accepted a cup of coffee and made stilted conversation with the old lady while I drank. When I finished I said, 'I'd like a word with Jack sometime.'

'He's out front,' she said.

'Oh?'

She let me go and seek him out myself while she attended to the cooking. He was slumped in an armchair in the sitting room, a couple of unopened Sunday papers beside him. He held a drink and stared out through the double-glazed windows at the rain. He half-turned when he heard the door opening.

'Is that you, Brian? Help yourself.'

'I've had coffee with Mrs Gorman. I brought Deirdre back.'

'She all right?'

I hesitated. 'A bit off colour, we thought.'

'In what way?' His voice was sharp.

'She seemed to be having quite a few nightmares.'

'Anything else?'

'Nothing really. Just one or two little things that seemed to indicate she isn't quite herself.'

He wanted to know exactly. He was insistent, so I told him.

'I thought if she got away from the family she might be better . . .'

'What's the matter with her?'

'Do you really want to know?' He immediately began to tell me at length the things he hadn't discussed with the family doctor, the psychiatrist or the priest. (But later on I ran into a couple of people who had heard the same story from him.) After he had talked for a bit I accepted a drink, and by the end of the morning we had killed the bottle.

He said that the holiday had gone very well – for most of the time. No problems going down, apart from the odd child getting car sick. They went right to the west end of the Dingle peninsula where a farmer near Dunquin rented them a site in a small stonewalled field. There was a view of the sea across the Blaskets towards the pointed peaks of the Skelligs eight or nine miles to the south. The same view they kept showing in *Ryan's Daughter*. The Sprite was a great success – the interior very clean, made more so by Breda. Deirdre and the babies slept in it with their parents, while the two boys had a tent. The weather was perfect and they worked out a routine. Every morning Jack would take all the children down the lane to Krugers to shop while Breda made up the bunks, cleaned the sinkful of Tupperware and put the washing to soak. After that most days they went to some beach for a picnic. Jack fitted in a good bit of golf. The boys played football while Deirdre spent a lot of time on a school project – collecting shells, or wild flowers which she put in jam-jars or pressed in books.

The sun never stopped shining. A couple of days before they left, the wind died altogether and it became too hot, even in the early morning. The air was stagnant, the sea looked like glue, the Blaskets were turned into sea monster's humps. As they sat round the greasy breakfast plates, the curtains were drawn to keep out the sun.

The boys were shouting for football, while Deirdre wrote neat labels. Breda had a naggy look similar to Deirdre's air of concentration. She was needling Jack about his golf and the round of drinks afterwards that kept him away from his beloved family which would soon be going back to school. Once term began they would see less of their Daddy. He gave in without too much reluctance, because of the heat. He'd made no firm commitment to play. So they got off quite early that day on their picnic.

They left Dunquin, driving past the little mound that is known as Uaig Ri na Spainne – the Grave of the Sun of the King of Spain – under Mount Eagle and the black claw of Dunmore Head to Coumeenole Bay. About a half dozen other holiday families were there already. They joined them, taking down the baskets, rugs and newspapers. Jack put up canvas chairs for himself and Breda and erected the canvas windbreak, more to create a patch of shade than anything. The little white beach, facing-south-west, shimmered against the glaring blue of the sunlit water.

Jack and the children swam while Breda cut the bread and divided up the ham and tomatoes and hardboiled eggs, and poured orange squash into plastic mugs. After they had eaten, the parents had their flask of coffee while the children received their daily handout of sweets. Then the elder ones drifted off.

'No more swimming for now,' Jack called as they made their way down to the limp wave line. Breda, wearing dark glasses, read the paper. The babies, in sun hats, pottered near her. Jack slapped lotion on himself.

When he first heard Deirdre's cries he knew it was her straightaway. Sitting up in the glare he looked over the windbreak; he could only pick out two members of his family from the figures strewn along the beach. The boys were standing beside their football which was only visible against the sand because of its hexagonal black markings.

He thought she must be drowning. 'My God, where is she?' He looked seawards; in the distance he could see the fuzzy shape of the Great Blasket, and between it and him the oily current flowing over the Stromboli rocks in a way that seemed to set them moving. He searched the shoreline. The cries were difficult to pinpoint, but people were looking round.

'There!' Breda shrieked. He felt nothing but relief when he located her at last. In fact she was well away from the water, up above the tide mark, a plump little figure standing with her hands over her eyes making this terrible racket. He ran over, Breda gathering up babies and following more slowly. When he got to where she was, her mouth was still wide open in a gape and her eyes were still covered with her hands.

'What is it, darling?' Taking her in his arms, he looked for cuts from broken glass. He had to shout to make himself heard. He couldn't see any blood.

'Stop them!'

'Stop what, treasure?'

'Stop the killing.'

He carried her back towards Breda. A couple of people looked up curiously as Deirdre's wails, making a counterpoint to the song on their transistor, passed them. Gradually her sobs subsided into sniffs and gasps. Once, though, she cried out suddenly, 'They're screaming, Daddy.'

Breda could do nothing with her. She'd be quiet for a bit and then start crying again. She was attracting attention so that in the end they collected everything and drove back. Jack gave up the idea of golf and endured the atmosphere in the stifling caravan for the rest of the day. The babies were fractious, the boys quarrelled and Deirdre sat huddled on a bunk. Breda thought she might have spot of sunstroke, but her temperature was normal. Between the fits of sobbing she was almost silent, answering her parents in monosyllables without even a 'Mummy' or 'Daddy' tacked on. If they tried to question her the crying was worse. That night was the first in which she kept calling out in her sleep.

Next day Jack took the boys off, leaving Breda to pack. Deirdre insisted on staying behind with the babies. She did her own version of packing by taking her jam-jars of shells and carrying them over to a ruined cabin that stood on the edge of the field. She threw them all in among the nettles. When Jack was collecting his things together he missed the good leather-handled hammer from his tool-box. He found it easily enough not far from the Sprite, lying beside a stone on which there were the crumbling remains of a substance which he identified as coral from a big piece Deirdre had found on a beach a week before. Stuck to some of it was a piece of lead that had once been round, but was now flattened by blows of the hammer.

When they got back to Dublin Deirdre continued to be difficult. Sometimes she seemed to improve, but then it would be the same thing all over again. The night the weather broke with a thunderstorm she screamed so loudly that a neighbour heard and complained. Her teacher telephoned specially to inquire what was wrong. The family doctor recommended a psychiatrist; there was something of reproach in the hectoring questions he asked them.

'I think his hint that it was all our fault finally drove Breda over the edge.' Jack filled up our glasses. 'He couldn't even make anything out of the drawings.'

'What drawings?'

'I'll show you.' He went over the nylon carpet with its bright pattern of pinwheels to the bookshelf on the right of the rough stone fireplace. Searching among the Reader's Digest condensations, Leon Uris's *Trinity* reverently displayed as if it were indeed a holy book, and the Harold Robbins and Arthur Haileys, he pulled out a stack of library books and finally the AA Book on Ireland, which had a wad of papers in it.

'When she got home she did nothing for a few days and then she began to draw. The same thing, time and again. Of course drawings are meat and drink to these boys and he was very interested. He said to encourage her – that drawing would provide a form of therapy which would help her work out her trauma. He asked if Deirdre was a particularly imaginative child in my opinion. Would you say Deirdre was imaginative?'

'No.' He had spread out a number of papers on the coffee table. They showed a crude child's version of an old-fashioned sailing ship with four masts, a high poop, gunports and flags. It looked very battered.

'He was particularly interested in the torn sails and the crack in the hull. He said that distressed children often convey their feelings in drawings. Most kids like to draw trees and houses. If they do a tree . . . the roots represent the id, the trunk the ego, and the top the super ego.'

'What's that supposed to mean?'

'Jung and his people worked it all out. If the tree is emphasized rather than the roots the child is living in a fantasy world. Look at these ships, the way they float over the waves.'

I looked at them carefully. 'She might just have been trying to convey the effects of a storm.'

'You or I might think so. Not that laddo. He said that a child who has had a traumatic experience within its own family will often draw its house with a crack in it. And sometimes it will put in curtained windows – or cover the windows completely – that is another distress signal. And if it draws trees, another very common theme, they will often have boles which are very much emphasized. Often they will have smoke coming out of them. So your man interpreted these black portholes, and the little bit of smoke at the end of the cannon here and there, and the broken mast and torn sails and all the rest as interesting variations on usual run of the mill disturbed drawings. And he kept asking if Breda and I had had any significant disagreements over the holiday which might have affected the child. It wasn't until a couple of days after I saw him that I realized what nonsense he was talking and that what Deirdre was drawing was a lot of pictures of the *Santa Maria de la Rosa*.'

The books he had with him were Garrett Mattingly's *Defeat of the Spanish Armada*, Evelyn Hardy's *Survivors of the Armada* and Rober Stenuit's *Treasures of the Armada*. He first opened up the AA book and found an article on marine archaeology which had a clear little diagrammatic illustration. 'For a time I thought Deirdre was just copying from here. Look, she has the same details, the flags and pennant of the Vice Flag Ship of the squadron. And all the different shapes of the sails are right – I've checked. You can make them out, even though she has them torn. All except the foresail. And one mast broken. In every picture.'

His eyes looked glazed. 'She got it all right.' Now he was referring to passages in the library books marked with dog-eared pages. 'On 13 September 1588 two great ships came down the west coast to just off the Blaskets. They were galleons called the *San Juan de Portugal* and the *San Juan Bautista*. These were two that got away. They anchored for a time, and later set off again, and in the end they got back to Spain. But before that could happen there was a hell of a storm.'

He was referring to another book. 'This storm was on the 21st of September. It swept two other Spanish ships into the sound. One of them was the *Santa Maria de la Rosa*. She was a Mediterranean merchantman that had been specially converted for the Armada. She displaced 945 tons and carried 26 guns. She had a complement of 64 sailors and 233 soldiers. Plenty of gentlemen and proud Spanish hidalgos among them.'

I accepted another glass. He was taking his neat. 'At midday on the 21st she came into the sound nearer land on the north-west side. She fired a shot on entering as if seeking help, and another further on. All her sails were in pieces except the foresail. She anchored, but the anchor dragged and she struck the Stromboli rocks. She sank with all hands, just about.'

'How do they know all this?'

The captain of the *San Juan Bautista* gave a deposition when he got home to Spain.' He paused. 'I'll tell you a thing about Deirdre. If you try and question her directly it's all dreams and nightmares. But if you ask her about the drawings she doesn't mind. She's usually quite pleased to answer. What do you make of this one?'

He pushed over another sketch of a sailing ship drawn with bright felt pens, the same as the others except that in the wavy blue sea was a black figure with its arms raised.

'When I asked her about him she said, 'That's Juan.' And I said, 'One what?' And she said, very angry. 'Not one. Juan. Hoo-an. He's not going to be drowned.' That's when I went to the library.' He opened up another reference. 'Seemingly there was just one survivor. They captured him, and before they hanged him he gave evidence.' He read out: 'His ship broke against the rocks in the sound of the Bleskies a league and half from land

upon the Tuesday at noon, and all in the ship perished
saving this examinate, who saved himself upon two or
three planks . . .'

'Oh come on, Jack, she's having you on . . . She's read
about it somewhere.'

'She can only just read.'

'Well then, she's learnt about it at school.'

'Breda and I have had to have a couple of sessions with
Miss Synott. I asked her specifically if the class had
learned anything about the Armada. No, nothing.'

'What about television then?'

'It's possible.' He hardly considered it. 'Here's another,
just to show you.' The ship with its torn sails and shattered
hull was drawn with a curve of shoreline on which some
big curly waves were breaking. The sand, violently yellow,
was scattered with what seemed to be piles of black sticks
or seaweed.

'No, not seaweed. I asked her. Bodies, she said.'

The last picture he showed me was done with a black
pen, and the lack of colour gave it an odd authenticity.
This time the little figures had been drawn with great
care, and some of them were good enough to put you in
mind of Derricke's engravings in the *Image of Ireland*.
Jack pointed out details as if it were a holiday snapshot.

'Here's poor old Giovanni or Juan on his gallows in this
corner. And this is a group of local militia. These are the
Spaniards they are killing.'

The two groups took up the centre of the page, the
people on the right thrusting swords into those on the left.
Several of the left-hand people were lying prone, within
reach of a couple of men bending over them.

'They're stripping them of jewels and weapons.'

'But who are the ones being killed? I thought you said
that Giovanni was the only survivor from the *Santa Maria
de la Rosa*?'

'He's the only one mentioned in the history books.'

'Who are these supposed to be then?'

'They're more survivors. Deirdre saw them. They went unrecorded. There were thousands of Spaniards off Armada ships being slaughtered all round the west coast, right? When it came to writing down what happened plenty of incidents like this must have been missed out. Giovanni gave evidence that a party went ashore from the *Santa Maria* to try and find water. There's no definite mention of their return. And the captain of the *San Juan Bautista* testified that two days before the storm Admiral Recalde, who was on board his ship, put fifty men ashore in an attempt to get supplies, but they were turned back by some soldiers. He wrote: "100 arquebusiers were marching, bearing a white standard with a red cross. It was concluded that they were English."'

'It seems unlikely they would have waited around for two days.'

'Not at all. We happen to know that there was a detachment of English soldiers at the west end of the Dingle peninsula. It was commanded by a man called James Trent, one of the Sovereign of Dingle's officers. His job was to watch over the Spanish ships anchored off Great Blasket Island. He actually wrote a letter in which he said, "We have two hundred men watching upon the shore every day. We stand in no fear of them" – he meant the Spanish – "for they are so much afraid for themselves". It's clear that Captain Trent's men did a little killing that never made the lists. Look.' Jack showed me another of Deirdre's pictures – a small group of soldiers, three of whom held old-fashioned guns with trumpet-like barrels. 'Arquebuses.' Another carried a standard with a red cross. It was the only bit of colour in the whole picture.

'I must go,' I said. 'Lunch will be waiting.'

WILLIAM TREVOR

The Raising of Elvira Tremlett

My mother preferred English goods to Irish, claiming that the quality was better. In particular she had a preference for English socks and vests, and would not be denied in her point of view. Irish motor-car assemblers made a rough-and-ready job of it, my father used to say, the Austins and Morrises and Vauxhalls that came direct from British factories were twice the cars. And my father was an expert in his way, being the town's single garage-owner. *Devlin Bros*. it said on a length of painted wood, black letters on peeling white. The sign was crooked on the red corrugated iron of the garage, falling down a bit on the left-hand side.

In all other ways my parents were intensely of the country that had borne them, of the province of Munster and of the town they had always known. When she left the Presentation convent my mother had been found employment in the meat factory, working a machine that stuck labels on to tins. My father and his brother Jack, finishing at the Christian Brothers, had automatically passed into the family business. In those days the only sign on the corrugated façade had said *Raleigh Cycles*, for the business, founded by my grandfather, had once been a bicycle one. 'I think we'll make a change in that,' my father annouced one day in 1933 when I was five, and six months or so later the rusty tin sheet that advertised bicycles was removed, leaving behind an island of grey in the corrugated red. 'Ah, that's grand,' my mother approved from the middle of the street, wiping her chapped hands on her apron. The new sign must have had a freshness and gleam on it, but I don't recall that. In my memory there is only the peeling white behind the letters and the drooping down at the left-hand side where a rivet had fallen out. 'We'll paint that in and we'll be dandy,' my Uncle Jack said, referring to the island that remained, the contours of Sir Walter Raleigh's head and shoulders. But the job was never done.

We lived in a house next door to the garage, two storeys of cement that had a damp look, with green window-sashes and a green hall-door. Inside, a wealth of polished brown linoleum, its pattern faded to nothing, was cheered here and there by the rugs my mother bought in Roche's Stores in Cork. The votive light of a crimson Sacred Heart gleamed day and night in the hall. Christ blessed us half-way up the stairs; on the landing the Virgin Mary was coy in garish robes. On the side of a narrow trodden carpet the staircase had been grained to make it seem like oak. In the dining room, never used, there was a square table with six rexine-seated chairs around it, and over the mantelpiece a mirror with chromium decoration. The sitting room smelt of must and had a picture of the Pope.

The kitchen was where everything happened. My father and Uncle Jack read the newspaper there. The old Philips wireless, the only one in the house, stood on one of the window-sills. Our two nameless cats used to crouch by the door into the scullery because one of them had once caught a mouse there. Our terrier, Tom, mooched about under my mother's feet when she was cooking at the range. There was a big scrubbed table in the middle of the kitchen, and wooden chairs, and a huge clock, like the top bit of a grandfather clock, hanging between the two windows. The dresser had keys and bits of wire and labels hanging all over it. The china it contained was never used, being hidden behind bric-à-brac: broken

ornaments left there in order to be repaired with Secco-
tine, worn-out parts from the engines of cars which my
father and uncle had brought into the kitchen to examine
at their leisure, bills on spikes, letters and Christmas
cards. The kitchen was always rather dusky, even in the
middle of the day: it was partially a basement, light
penetrating from outside only through the upper panes of
its two long windows. Its concrete floor had been red-
dened with Cardinal polish, which was renewed once a
year, in spring. Its walls and ceiling were a sooty white.

The kitchen was where we did our homework, my two
sisters and two brothers and myself. I was the youngest,
my brother Cathal the oldest. Cathal and Liam were
destined for the garage when they finished at the Christian
Brothers, as my father and Uncle Jack had been. My
sister Effie was good at arithmetic and the nuns had once
or twice mentioned accountancy. There was a commercial
college in Cork she could go to, the nuns said, the same
place that Miss Madden who did the books for Bolger's
Medical Hall had attended. Everyone said my sister Kitty
was pretty: my father used to take her on his knee and
tell her she'd break some fellow's heart, or a dozen hearts
or maybe more. She didn't know what he was talking
about at first, but later she understood and used to go red
in the face. My father was like that with Kitty. He
embarrassed her without meaning to, hauling her on to
his knee when she was much too old for it, fondling her
because he liked her best. On the other hand, he was
quite harsh with my brothers, constantly suspicious that
they were up to no good. Every evening he asked them if
they'd been to school that day, suspecting that they might
have tricked the Christian Brothers and would the next
day present them with a note they had written themselves,
saying they'd had stomach trouble after eating bad sausages. He and my Uncle Jack had often engaged in such

ploys themselves, spending a whole day in the field behind the electricity plant, smoking Woodbines.

My father's attitude to my sister Effie was coloured by Effie's plainness. 'Ah, poor old Effie,' he used to say, and my mother would reprimand him. He took comfort from the fact that if the garage continued to thrive it would be necessary to have someone doing the increased bookwork instead of himself and Uncle Jack trying to do it. For this reason he was in favour of Effie taking a commercial course: he saw a future in which she and my two brothers would live in the house and run the business between them. One or other of my brothers would marry and maybe move out of the house, leaving Effie and whichever one would still be a bachelor: it was my father's way of coming to terms with Effie's plainness. 'I wonder if Kitty'll end up with young Lacy?' I once heard him inquiring of my mother, the Lacy he referred to being the only child of another business in the town – Geo. Lacy and Sons, High-Class Drapers – who was about eight at the time. Kitty would do well, she'd marry whom she wanted to, and somehow or other she'd marry money: he really believed that.

For my part I fitted in nowhere in my father's vision of the family's future. My performance at school was poor and there would be no place for me in the garage. I used to sit with the others at the kitchen table trying to understand algebra and Irish grammar, trying without any hope to learn verses from 'The Lady of Shalott' and to improve my handwriting by copying from a headline book. 'Slow,' Brother Flynn had reported. 'Slow as a dying snail, that boy is.'

That was the family we were. My father was bulky in his grey overalls, always with marks of grease or dirt on him, his fingernails rimmed with black, like fingers in mourning, I used to think. Uncle Jack wore similar overalls but he was thin and much smaller than my father, a ferrety little man, who had a way of looking at the ground when he spoke to you. He, too, was marked with grime and had the same rimmed fingernails, even at weekends. They both brought the smell of the garage into the kitchen, an oily smell that mingled with the fumes of my uncle's pipe and my father's cigarettes.

My mother was red-cheeked and stout, with wavy black hair and big arms and legs. She ruled the house, and was often cross: with my brothers when they behaved obstreperously, with my sisters and myself when her patience failed her. Sometimes my father would spend a long time on a Saturday night in Keogh's, which was the public house he favoured, and she would be cross with him also, noisily shouting in their bedroom, telling him to take off his clothes before he got into bed, telling him he was a fool. Uncle Jack was a teetotaller, a member of the Pioneer movement. He was a great help to Canon O'Keefe in the rectory and in the Church of the Holy Assumption, performing chores and repairing the electric light. Twice a year he spent a Saturday night in Cork in order to go to greyhound racing, but there was more than met the eye to these visits, for on his return there was always a great silence in the house, a fog of disapproval emanating from my father.

The first memories I have are of the garage, of watching my father and Uncle Jack at work, sparks flying from the welding apparatus, the dismantling of oil-caked engines. A car would be driven over the pit and my father or uncle would work underneath it, lit by an electric bulb in a wire casing on the end of a flex. Often, when he wasn't in the pit, my father would drift into conversation with a customer. He'd lean on the bonnet of a car, smoking continuously, talking about a hurling match that had taken place or about the dishonesties of the government.

He would also talk about his children, saying that Cathal and Liam would fit easily into the business and referring to Effie's plans to study commerce, and Kitty's prettiness. 'And your man here?' the customer might remark, inclining his head in my direction. To this question my father always replied in the same way. The Lord, he said, would look after me.

As I grew up I became aware that I made both my father and my mother uneasy. I assumed that this was due to my slowness at school, an opinion that was justified by a conversation I once overheard coming from their bedroom: they appeared to regard me as mentally deficient. My father repeated twice that the Lord would look after me. It was something she prayed for, my mother replied, and I imagined her praying after she'd said it, kneeling down by their bed, as she'd taught all of us to kneel by ours. I stood with my bare feet on the linoleum of the landing, believing that a plea from my mother was rising from the house at that very moment, up into the sky where God was. I had been on my way to the kitchen for a drink of water, but I returned to the bedroom I shared with Cathal and Liam and lay awake thinking of the big brown-brick mansion on the Mallow road. Once it had been owned and lived in by a local family. Now it was the town's asylum.

The town itself was small and ordinary. Part of it was on a hill, the part where the slum cottages were, where three or four shops had nothing in their windows except pasteboard advertisements for tea and Bisto. The rest of the town was flat, a single street with one or two narrow streets running off it. Where they met there was a square of a kind, with a statue of Daniel O'Connell. The Munster and Leinster Bank was here, and the Bank of Ireland, and Lacy and Sons, and Bolger's Medical Hall, and the Home and Colonial. Our garage was at one end of the main street, opposite Corrigan's Hotel. The Electric Cinema was at the other, a stark white façade, not far from the Christian Brothers, the convent and the Church of the Holy Assumption. The Protestant church was at the top of the hill, beyond the slums.

When I think of the town now I can see it very clearly: cattle and pigs on a fair day, always a Monday; Mrs Driscoll's vegetable shop. Vickery's hardware, Phelan's the barber's, Kilmartin's the turf accountant's, the convent and the Christian Brothers, twenty-nine public houses. The streets are empty on a sunny afternoon, there's a smell of bread. Brass plates gleam on the way home from school: Dr Thos. Garvey MD, RCS, Regan and O'Brien Commissioners for Oaths, W. Tracy Dental Surgeon.

But in my thoughts our house and our garage close in on everything else, shadowing and diminishing the town. The bedroom I shared with Cathal and Liam had the same nondescript linoleum as the hall and the landing had. There was a dressing-table with a wash-stand in white-painted wood, and a wardrobe that matched. There was a flowery wallpaper on the walls, but the flowers had all faded to a uniform brown, except behind the bedroom's single picture, of an ox pulling a cart. Our three iron bedsteads were lined against one wall. Above the mantelpiece Christ on his cross had already given up the ghost.

I didn't in any way object to this bedroom and, familiar with no alternative, I didn't mind sharing it with my brothers. The house itself was somewhere I was used to also, accepted and taken for granted. But the garage was different. The garage was a kind of hell, its awful earth floor made black with sump oil, its huge indelicate vices, the chill of cast iron, the grunting of my father and my uncle as they heaved an engine out of a tractor, the cloying smell of petrol. It was there that my silence, my dumbness almost, must have begun. I sense that now, without being able accurately to remember. Looking back, I see myself silent in a classroom, taught first by nuns and later by Christian Brothers. In the kitchen, while the others chattered at mealtimes, I was silent too. I could take no interest in what my father and uncle reported about the difficulties they were having in getting spare parts or about some fault in a farmer's carburettor. My brothers listened to all that, and clearly found it easy to. Or they would talk about sport, or tease Uncle Jack about the money he lost on greyhounds and horses. My mother would repeat what she had heard in the shops, and Uncle Jack would listen intently because although he never himself indulged in gossip he loved to hear it. My sister would retail news from the convent, the decline in the health of an elderly nun, or the inability of some family to buy Lacy's more expensive First Communion dresses. I often felt, listening at mealtimes, that I was scarcely there. I didn't belong and I sensed it was my fault; I felt I was a burden, being slow and unpromising at school, unable to hold out hopes for the future. I felt I was a disgrace to them and might even become a person who was only fit to lift cans of paraffin about in the garage. I thought I could see that in my father's eyes, and in my uncle's sometimes, and in my mother's. A kind of shame it was, peering back at me.

I turned to Elvira Tremlett because everything about her was quiet. 'You great damn clown,' my mother would shout angrily at my father. He'd smile in the kitchen, swaying and red-faced, smelling like a brewery, as she used to say. 'Mind that bloody tongue of yours,' he'd retort, and then he'd eye my uncle in a belligerent manner. 'Jeez, will you look at the cut of him?' he'd roar, laughing and throwing his head about. My uncle would usually be sitting in front of the range, a little to one side so as not to be in the way of my mother while she cooked. He'd been reading the *Independent* or *Ireland's Own*, or trying to mend something. 'You're the right eejit,' my father would say to him. 'And the right bloody hypocrite.'

It was always like that when he'd been in Keogh's on a Saturday evening and returned in time for his meal. My mother would slap the plates on to the table, my father would sing in order to annoy her. I used to feel that my uncle and my mother were allied on these occasions, just as she and my father were allied when my uncle spent a Saturday night in Cork after the greyhound racing. I much preferred it when my father didn't come back until some time in the middle of the night. 'Will you look at His Nibs?' he'd say in the kitchen, drawing attention to me. 'Haven't you a word in you, boy? Bedad, that fellow'll never make a lawyer.' He'd explode with laughter and then he'd tell Kitty that she was looking great and could marry the crowned King of England if she wanted to. He'd say to Effie she was getting fat with the toffees she ate; he'd tell my brothers they were lazy.

They didn't mind his talk the way I did; even Kitty's embarrassment used to evaporate quite quickly because for some reason she was fond of him. Effie was fond of my uncle and my brothers of my mother. Yet in spite of all this family feeling, whenever there was quarrelling between our parents or an atmosphere after my uncle had spent a night away my brothers used to say the three of them would drive you mad. 'Wouldn't it make you sick, listening to it?' Cathal would say in our bedroom, saying it to Liam. Then they'd laugh because they couldn't be bothered to concern themselves too much with other people's quarrels, or with atmospheres.

The fact was, my brothers and sister were all part of it,

whatever it was – the house, the garage, the family we were – and they could take everything in their stride. They were the same as our parents and our uncle, and Elvira Tremlett was different. She was a bit like Myrna Loy, whom I had seen in the Electric, in *Test Pilot* and *Too Hot to Handle* and *The Thin Man*. Only she was more beautiful than Myrna Loy, and her voice was nicer. Her voice, I still consider, was the nicest thing about Elvira Tremlett, next to her quietness.

'What do you want?' the sexton of the Protestant church said to me one Saturday afternoon. 'What're you doing here?'

He was an old hunched man in black clothes. He had rheumy eyes, very red and bloody at the rims. It was said in the town that he gave his wife an awful time.

'It isn't your church,' he said.

I nodded, not wanting to speak to him. He said:

'It's a sin for you to be coming into a Protestant church. Are you wanting to be a Protestant, is that it?' He was laughing at me, even though his lips weren't smiling. He looked as if he'd never smiled in his life.

I shook my head at him, hoping he might think I was dumb.

'Stay if you want to,' he said, surprising me, even though I'd seen him coming to the conclusion that I wasn't going to commit some act of vandalism. I think he might even have decided to be pleased because a Catholic boy had chosen to wander among the pews and brasses of his church. He hobbled away to the vestry, breathing noisily because of his bent condition.

Several months before that Saturday I had wandered into the church for the first time. It was different from the Church of the Holy Assumption. It had a different smell, a smell that might have come from mothballs or from the tidy stacks of hymn-books and prayer-books, whereas the Church of the Holy Assumption smelt of people and candles. It was cosier, much smaller, with dark-coloured panelling and pews, and stained-glass windows that seemed old, and no cross on the altar. There were flags and banners that were covered with dust, all faded and in shreds, and a bible spread out on the wings of an eagle.

The old sexton came back. I could feel him watching me as I read the tablets on the walls, moving from one to the next, pretending that each of them interested me. I might have asked him: I might have smiled at him and timidly inquired about Elvira Tremlett because I knew he was old enough to remember. But I didn't. I walked slowly up a side-aisle, away from the altar to the back of the church. I wanted to linger there in the shadows, but I could feel his rheumy eyes on my back, wondering about me. As I slipped away from the church, down the short path that led through black iron gates to the street at the top of the hill, I knew that I would never return to the place.

'Well, it doesn't matter,' she said. 'You don't have to go back. There's nothing to go back for.'

I knew that was true. It was silly to keep on calling in at the Protestant church.

'It's curiosity that sends you there,' she said. 'You're much too curious.'

I knew I was: she had made me understand that. I was curious and my family weren't.

She smiled her slow smile, and her eyes filled with it. Her eyes were brown, the same colour as her long hair. I loved it when she smiled. I loved watching her fingers playing with the daisies in her lap. I loved her old-fashioned clothes, and her shoes and her two elaborate earrings. She laughed once when I asked her if they were gold. She'd never been rich, she said.

There was a place, a small field with boulders in it, hidden on the edge of a wood. I had gone there the first time, after I'd been in the Protestant church. What had happened was that in the church I had noticed the tablet on the wall, the left wall as you faced the altar, the last tablet on it, in dull grey marble.

> Nearby this Stone
> Lies Interred the Body
> Of Miss Elvira Tremlett
> Daughter of Wm. Tremlett
> Of Tremlett Hall
> in the County of Dorset.
> She Departed this Life
> 30 August 1873
> Aged 18.

Why should an English girl die in our town? Had she been passing through? Had she died of poisoning? Had someone shot her? Eighteen was young to die.

On that day, the first day I read her tablet, I had walked from the Protestant church to the field beside the wood. I often went there because it was a lonely place, away from the town and from people. I sat on a boulder and felt hot sun on my face and head, and on my neck and the backs of my hands. I began to imagine her, Elvira Tremlett of Tremlett Hall in the country of Dorset, England. I gave her her long hair and her smile and her elaborate earrings, and I felt I was giving her gifts. I gave her her clothes, wondering if I had got them right. Her fingers were delicate as straws, lacing together the first of her daisy-chains. Her voice hadn't the edge that Myrna Loy's had, her neck more elegant.

'Oh, love,' she said on the Saturday after the sexton had spoken to me. 'The tablet's only a stone. It's silly to go gazing at it.'

I knew it was and yet it was hard to prevent myself. The more I gazed at it the more I felt I might learn about her. I didn't know if I was getting her right. I was afraid even to begin to imagine her death because I thought I might be doing wrong to have her dying from some cause that wasn't the correct one. It seemed insulting to her memory not to get that perfectly right.

'You mustn't want too much,' she said to me on that Saturday afternoon. 'It's as well you've finished with the tablet on the wall. Death doesn't matter, you know.'

I never went back to the Protestant church. I remember what my mother had said about the quality of English goods, and how cars assembled in England were twice the ones as those assembled in Dublin. I looked at the map of England in my atlas and there was Dorset. She'd been travelling, maybe staying in a house near by, and had died somehow: she was right, it didn't matter.

Tremlett Hall was by a river in the country, with Virginia creeper all over it, with long corridors and suits of armour in the hall, and a fireplace in the hall also. In *David Copperfield*, which I had seen in the Electric, there might have been a house like Tremlett Hall, or in *A Yank at Oxford*: I couldn't quite remember. The gardens were beautiful: you walked from one garden to another, to a special rosegarden with a sundial, a vegetable garden, with high walls around it. In the house someone was always playing a piano. 'Me,' Elvira said.

My brothers went to work in the garage, first Cathal and then Liam. Effie went to Cork, to the commercial college. The boys at the Christian Brothers began to whistle at Kitty and sometimes would give me notes to pass on to her. Even when other people were there I could feel Elvira's nearness, even her breath sometimes, and certainly the warmth of her hands. When Brother Flynn hit me one day she cheered me up. When my father came back from Keogh's in time for his Saturday tea her presence made it easier. The garage I hated, where I was certain now I would one day lift paraffin cans from one corner to another, was lightened by her. She was in Mrs Driscoll's vegetable shop when I bought cabbage and potatoes for my mother. She was there while I waited for the Electric to open, and when I walked through the animals on a fair day. In the stony field the sunshine made her earrings glitter. It danced over a brooch she had not had when first I imagined her, a brooch with a scarlet jewel, in the shape of a dragon. Mist caught in her hair, wind ruffled the skirts of her old-fashioned dress. She wore gloves when it was cold, and a green cloak that wrapped itself all around her. In spring she often carried daffodils, and once – one Sunday in June – she carried a little dog, a grey Cairn that afterwards became part of her, like her earrings and her brooch.

I grew up but she was always eighteen, as petrified as her tablet on the wall. In the bedroom which I shared with Cathal and Liam I came, in time, to take her dragon's brooch from her throat and to take her earrings from her pale ears and to lift her dress from her body. Her limbs were warm, and her smile was always there. Her slender fingers traced caresses on my cheeks. I told her that I loved her, as the people told one another in the Electric.

'You know why they're afraid of you?' she said one day in the field by the wood. 'You know why they hope that God will look after you?'

I had to think about it but I could come to no conclusion on my own, without her prompting. I think I wouldn't have dared: I'd have been frightened of whatever there was.

'You know what happens,' she said, 'when your uncle stays in Cork on a Saturday night? You know what happened once when your father came back from Keogh's too late for his meal, in the middle of the night?'

I knew before she told me. I guessed, but I wouldn't have if she hadn't been there. I made her tell me, listening to her quiet voice. My Uncle Jack went after women as well as greyhounds in Cork. It was his weakness, like going to Keogh's was my father's. And the two weaknesses had once combined, one Saturday night a long time ago when my uncle hadn't gone to Cork and my father was a long time in Keogh's. I was the child of my uncle Jack and my mother, born of his weakness and my mother's anger as she waited for the red bleariness of my father to return, footless in the middle of the night. It was why my father called my uncle a hypocrite. It was maybe why my uncle was always looking at the ground, and why he assisted Canon O'Keefe in the rectory and in the Church of the Holy Assumption. I was their sin, growing in front of them, for God to look after.

'They have made you,' Elvira said. 'The three of them have made you what you are.'

I imagined my father returning that night from Keogh's stumbling on the stairs, and haste being made by my uncle to hide himself. In these images it was always my uncle who was anxious and in a hurry: my mother kept saying it didn't matter, pressing him back on to the pillows, wanting him to be found there.

My father was like a madman in the bedroom then, wild in his crumpled Saturday clothes. He struck at both of them, his befuddled eyes tormented while my mother screamed. She went back through all the years of their marriage, accusing him of cruelty and neglect. My uncle wept. 'I'm no more than an animal to you,' my mother screamed, half-naked between the two of them. 'I cook and clean and have children for you. You give me thanks by going out to Keogh's.' Cathal was in the room, attracted by the noise. He stood by the open door, five years old, telling them to be quiet because they were waking the others.

'Don't ever tell a soul,' Cathal would have said, years afterwards, retailing that scene for Liam and Effie and Kitty, letting them guess the truth. He had been sent back to bed, and my uncle had gone to his own bed, and in the morning there had begun the pretending that none of it had happened. There was confession and penance, and extra hours spent in Keogh's. There were my mother's prayers that I would not be born, and my uncle's prayers, and my father's bitterness when the prayers weren't answered.

On the evening of the day that Elvira shared all that with me I watched them as we ate in the kitchen, my father's hands still smeared with oil, his fingernails in mourning, my uncle's eyes bent over his fried eggs. My brothers and sisters talked about events that had taken place in the town; my mother listened without interest, her large round face seeming stupid to me now. It was a cause for celebration that I was outside the family circle. I was glad not to be part of the house and the garage, not to be part of the town with its statue and its shops and its twenty-nine public houses. I belonged with a figment of my imagination, to an English ghost who had acquired a dog, whose lips were soft, whose limbs were warm, Elvira Tremlett who lay beneath the Protestant church.

'Oh, love,' I said in the kitchen, 'thank you.'

The conversation ceased, my father's head turned sharply. Cathal and Liam looked at me, so did Effie and Kitty. My mother had a piece of fried bread on a fork, on the way to her mouth. She returned it to her plate. There was grease at the corner of her lips, a little shiny stream from some previous mouthful, running down to her chin.

My uncle pushed his knife and fork together and stared at them.

I felt them believing with finality now, with proof, that I was not sane. I was fifteen years old, a boy who was slow and backward in his ways, who was all of a sudden addressing someone who wasn't in the room.

My father cut himself a slice of bread, moving the breadsaw slowly through the loaf. My brothers were as valuable in the garage now as he or my uncle; Effie kept the books and sent out bills. My father took thing easy, spending more time talking to his older customers. My uncle perused the racing pages; my mother had had an operation for varicose veins, which she should have had years ago.

I could disgrace them in the town, in all the shops and public houses, in Bolger's Medical Hall, in the convent and the Christian Brothers and the Church of the Holy Assumption. How could Cathal and Liam carry on the business if they couldn't hold their heads up? How could Effie help with the petrol pumps at a busy time, standing in her Wellington boots on a wet day, for all the town to see? Who would marry Kitty now?

I had spoken by mistake, and I didn't speak again. It was the first time I had said anything at a meal in the kitchen for as long as I could remember, for years and years. I had suddenly felt that she might grow tired of coming into my mind and want to be left alone, buried beneath the Protestant church. I had wanted to reassure her.

'They're afraid of you,' she said that night. 'All of them.'

She said it again when I walked in the sunshine to our field. She kept on saying it, as if to warn me, as if to tell me to be on the look-out. 'They have made you,' she repeated. 'You're the child of all of them.'

I wanted to go away, to escape from the truth we had both instinctively felt and had shared. I walked with her through the house called Tremlitt Hall, haunting other people with our footsteps. We stood and watching while guests at a party laughed among the suits of armour in the hall, while there was a waltzing in a ballroom. In the gardens dahlias bloomed, and sweet-peas clung to wires against a high stone wall. Low hedges of fuchsia bounded the paths among the flower-beds, the little dog ran on in front of us. She held my hand and said she loved me; she smiled at me in the sunshine. And then, just for a moment, she seemed to be different; she wasn't wearing the right clothes; she was wearing a tennis dress and had a racquet in her hand. She was standing in a conservatory, one foot on a cane chair. She looked like another girl, Susan Peters in *Random Harvest*.

I didn't like that. It was the same kind of thing as feeling I had to speak to her even though other people were in the kitchen. It was a muddle, and somewhere in it I could sense an unhappiness I didn't understand. I couldn't tell if it was hers or mine. I tried to say I was sorry, but I didn't know what I was sorry for.

In the middle of one night I woke up screaming. Cathal and Liam were standing by my bed, cross with me for waking them. My mother came, and then my father. I was still screaming, unable to stop. 'He's had some type of nightmare,' Cathal said.

It wasn't a nightmare because it continued when I was awake. She was there, Elvira Tremlett, born 1855. She didn't talk or smile: I couldn't make her. Something was failing in me: it was the same as Susan Peters suddenly appearing with a tennis racquet, the same as my desperation in wanting to show gratitude when we weren't in private.

My mother sat beside my bed. My brothers returned to theirs. The light remained on. I must have whispered, I must have talked about her because I remember my mother's nodding head and her voice assuring me that it was all a dream. I slept, and when I woke up it was light in the room and my mother had gone and my brothers were getting up. Elvira Tremlett was still there, one eye half-closed in blindness, the fingers that had been delicate misshapen now. When my brother left the room she was more vivid, a figure by the window, turning her head to look at me, a gleam of fury in her face. She did not speak but I knew what she was saying. I had used her for purposes of my own, to bring solace. What right, for God's sake, had I to blow life into her decaying bones? Born 1855, eighty-nine years of age.

I closed my eyes, trying to imagine her as I had before, willing her young girl's voice and her face and hair. But even with my eyes closed the old woman moved about the room, from the window to the foot of Liam's bed, to the wardrobe, into a corner, where she stood still.

She was on the landing with me, and on the stairs and in the kitchen. She was in the stony field by the wood, accusing me of disturbing her yet still not speaking. She was in pain from her eyes and her arthritic hands: I had brought about that. Yet she was no ghost. I knew she was no ghost. She was a figment of my imagination, drawn from her dull grey tablet by my interest. She existed within me, I told myself, but it wasn't a help.

Every night I woke up screaming. The sheets of my bed were sodden with my sweat. I would shout at my brothers and my mother, begging them to take her away from me. It wasn't I who had committed the sin, I shouted, it wasn't I who deserved the punishment. All I had done was to talk to a figment. All I'd done was to pretend, as they had.

Canon O'Keefe talked to me in the kitchen. His voice came and went, and my mother's voice spoke of the sheets sodden with sweat every morning, and my father's voice said there was terror in my eyes. All I wanted to say was that I hadn't meant any harm in raising Elvira Tremlett from the dead in order to have an imaginary friend, or in travelling with her to the house with Virginia creeper on it. She hadn't been real, she'd been no more than a flicker on the screen of the Electric Cinema: I wanted to say all that. I wanted to be listened to, to be released of the shame that I felt like a shroud around me. I knew that if I could speak my imagination would be free of the woman who haunted it now. I tried, but they were afraid of me. They were afraid of what I was going to say and between them they somehow stopped me. 'Our Father,' said Canon O'Keefe, 'Who art in heaven, Hallowed by Thy Name . . .'

Dr Garvey came and looked at me; in Cork another man looked at me. The man in Cork tried to make me talk to him, telling me to lie down, to take my shoes off if I wanted to. It wasn't any good, and it wasn't fair on them, having me there in the house, a person in some kind of nightmare. I quite see now that it wasn't fair on them, I quite see that.

Because of the unfairness I was brought, one Friday morning in a Ford car my father borrowed from a customer, to this brown-brick mansion, once the property of a local family. I have been here for thirty-five years. The clothes I wear are rough, but I have ceased to be visited by the woman whom Elvira Tremlett became, in my failing imagination. I ceased to be visited by her the moment I arrived here, for when that moment came I knew that this was the house she had been staying in when she died. She brought me here so that I could live in peace, even in the room that had been hers. I had disturbed her own peace so that we might come here together.

I have not told this story myself. It has been told by my weekly visitor, who has placed me at the centre of it because that, of course, is where I belong. Here, in the brown-red mansion, I have spoken without difficulty. I have spoken in the garden where I work in the daytime; I have spoken at all meals; I have spoken to my weekly visitor. I am different here. I do not need an imaginary friend, I could never again feel curious about a girl who died.

I have asked my visitor what they say in the town, and what the family say. He replies that in the bar of Corrigan's Hotel commercial travellers are told of a boy who was haunted, as a place or house is. They are drawn across the bar to a window: Devlin Bros., the garage across the street, is pointed out to them. They listen in pleasurable astonishment to the story of nightmares and hear the name of an English girl who died in the town in 1873, whose tablet is on the wall of the Protestant church. They were told of the final madness of the boy, which came about through his visions of this girl, Elvira Tremlett.

The story is famous in the town, the only story of its kind the town possesses. It is told as a mystery, and the strangers who hear it sometimes visit the Protestant church to look up at the tablet that commemorates a death in 1873. They leave the church in bewilderment, wondering why an uneasy spirit should have lighted on a boy so many years later. They never guess, not one of them, that the story as it happened wasn't a mystery in the least.

TERENCE DE VERE WHITE

One of the Family

'Mother, if you could see your Richard now!' was his final thought as he drove in his newly purchased car in his newly purchased riding clothes to his first hunt. He was passing the gate lodge of Ballyorney Park where she had been born and brought up and had left (in circumstances that had never been made perfectly clear to him) to marry his short-lived father, another dependent of the Templeton family, needless to say.

Ballyorney was a ruin now; the present Lord Templeton lived in the Isle of Man safeguarding what was left of the family fortune. The selection, signing and dispatching of a greeting card for him was the focal point of Christmas when Richard's mother was alive. When he gave up acknowledging them (with good wishes for the New Year) she absolved him from blame. No Templeton could do wrong; and, if one seemed to, you may be quite sure there were always extenuating circumstances.

Richard's first lesson from his mother in their two-roomed basement lodging was about the family. Before he could safety dispense with diapers he knew the names of the successive Templetons and their wives and children, as a precocious little English boy might his country's kings and queens. Lady Caroline, Lady Lucy, Lady Elisabeth, and many more – of these was composed his mother's litany of the saints. And in her pinching poverty her one regret was that there was no family now for her son, brought up in loyalty and reverence, to serve. With his brains and accomplishments and well-bred appearance he might even have been recommended to a bank or brewery by the reigning earl. She remembered how Lord Templeton's father was for ever having applications made to him by needy respectable people.

Although Ballyorney and the Templetons became eventually the whole matter of her conversation, his mother had only once taken Richard to visit her first home. The expedition was quite an enterprise, with a child of seven, and it took all of a wet Saturday getting there and back. The house he had pictured as a fairy castle had been burnt so thoroughly to the ground that now only a screen of granite with holes where windows should have been recalled its former glory. Ruined glass-houses in the garden where weeds were shoulder-high; roofless stables in the yard; paths choked with grass and moss; lily ponds coated by green slime – Ballyorney was depressing beyond belief. Those names that had sounded so arcadian when his mother recited them – the yew walk, Lady Caroline's garden, the top meadow – would stand in his mind henceforth as symbols of waste. For one sublime moment on that mournful day the sun came out, and he would never forget the paddock ablaze with scarlet poppies. These owed nothing to tradition. They shot up on their own. Fresh recruits for a defeated army.

Was it this experience – never repeated, never referred to – that freed him from the thraldom of generations to the Templetons? He would make his own world. His one memorable row with his mother took place when he began to show the flair for pictures which was to make him quite rich so quickly; she closed her eyes, rolled her head reminiscently, and said, 'I can hear Mr Charles.' He had great taste, she remembered, but married unfortunately. 'Am I never to do anything without your dragging in one of that bloody family?' he had blurted out then, and at once was sorry when he saw her face crumple. Blasphemy hurt her.

There was too much on his mind to allow him to dwell for long on nostalgia evoked by a bolted gate; if not exactly frightened, he was acutely nervous at the prospect ahead. It was one thing to show off at a riding-school, quite another to charge across country on a hired horse he had never seen or sat on before.

A mare – he knew enough to distinguish – she was waiting for him, saddled and bridled, with a girl at her head. Kind of eye and sleek of coat – the mare; he could not say as much for her attendant. With a nice economy she undermined the little confidence he was clinging to by telling him the hireling was 'a bit above herself and inclined to play up', and advised him to 'stand no nonsense if she was inclined to rear'. The horse-box would be waiting here at five o'clock, by which time the light would have gone in any event. She helped him into the saddle, slapped the mare on the neck, and slouched away. Richard would have gladly paid her to stay until the hunt moved off. The mare was as restless as a child in church, shaking her head up and down as if she hoped to escape from the bridle; embarrassing him by a way she had of half-turning and presenting her rear to passing traffic.

Why was he submitting himself to this trial by ordeal? To realize some fantasy? To give colour to a self-portrait he had in preparation? The gods have a short way with hubristic antics of this sort, and one of them was assessing his presumption, judging by the insolence of his stare when Richard was apologizing to a child with whose pony he had come into collision. A well-mounted man of Richard's own age – a stranger – but with something so familiar about his face that his failure to give any salute was painful. A humiliating admission. But for the moment

Richard wished himself anywhere else than ill-at-ease in a milling crowd of excited horses.

The horn sounded at last. The concourse sorted itself out; a general shuffle gradually became a procession; there was a jingling of harness and a hurry of hooves as the hunt moved out of the village.

On a side road the horses began to trot; then a halt while the Master put his horse at a ditch. Richard was hardly aware of how his own arrived eventually in a green expanse over which the pack was spread out, running fast, followed by the Master and his huntsman. Behind them came the lucky few who had avoided the pushing and cursing and apologizing that had dogged Richard's progress from road to field.

But now, seated firmly in the saddle, his mare's neck upright and steady at last, he found the cheerful pounding of her shoes on the firm turf sweeter than any music. Life will never be better than this. And his good feeling extended to the concentrated faces galloping beside him. At first there had been a good deal of overtaking when cavaliers who had been for some reason held back asserted the supremacy of their mounts; but by now a hierarchy had been established. Richard looked for the insolent witness of his incompetence but could not see him among the front runners.

Down one hill, up another; at the top, a fence – the first obstacle. Richard's heart stopped, but only for an instant. He must not let his mare feel the disquiet with which he looked between her ears at the barrier ahead. Over it went the hounds with swinging tails; the Master took it in the manner born; on his heels went three in a row. All over, safe and well. It was Richard's turn; the mare had seen the fence, and there was considerable reassurance in the asthmatic roar she gave, as if she had dealt with its like before. He let her have her head, and as she left the ground leaned forward, grasped her mane, closed his eyes, and offered up a short prayer. Before he was sure they had taken off, his bottom felt the reassuring pressure of the saddle, and the gallop proceeded as if there had been no interruption. And after that the jumps were like Atlantic breakers that carried him forward on their crest.

There were checks and delays and false scents by way of contrast. Richard looked for his recent enemy, but he was nowhere to be seen. He had either fallen or dropped out. He had a childish longing to return that stare with interest, having proved himself in the chase. He would not have admitted to himself that he would have liked to have been seen at the five-bar gate. It was incredible what a man can do when his blood is up if he has a brave animal beneath him.

Towards the end of the hunt, the hounds ran into a narrow lane; this led to crowding and confusion because the passage admitted only one rider at a time. Richard chafed at the delay; and, to rub it in, white clouds that had lain like snowdrifts on the edge of the blue began to move, losing their peaceful character in the process; thinning as they spread and turning black. A sour wind whipped up a shower of rain. The light suddenly began to fail; it was time for the harriers to pack it in. The mare appeared to think so; she began to shake her head about, and someone in a plaintive voice asked Richard to control his mount. The waiting transport was several miles away, and to crown the day's sport for the harriers a trail had been laid from where they were now congregating back to the village where they had met in the morning.

Richard had no inkling of this pleasure in store. He had dismounted to rest his mare when he caught a glimpse of the unfriendly horseman of the morning, looking as if neither he nor his horse had taken even the gentlest exercise in the meanwhile. He seemed to be trying to attract Richard's attention. When he was sure he had, he moved off on his horse, indicating by a motion of his head that he expected Richard to follow. He would have gone anywhere to get his animal moving again, even if he might not have cared to admit that he was flattered by this summons. To be noticed by someone who has aroused in one a feeling of inferiority is irresistible to vanity. In every hunt there is an experienced campaigner who insists on taking his own line; Richard assumed that he was being shown how to steal a march on the other riders.

The manoeuvre involved going back a few hundred yards and turning in the open gate of private grounds, an audacity which, judging by the horseman's mien, did not cost him a thought. He rode up to the house – it looked like a rectory – and went round it into a small yard where a wooden gate led into a field. Jumping the gate from a stand, without looking back, he set off at a furious pace across the field, which Richard remembered having passed through during the hunt. But now they were going across their original tracks. They had parted with the rest of the company. This was a *pas de deux*.

The leader was concentrating on keeping in front; Richard had expected him to make some companionable gesture when he saw that his invitation had been accepted. But he hadn't deigned to turn his head, and he was riding a fresher horse. They were now in a long field, at the end of which rose the wall of a demesne. It seemed to ensure an end to their mad gallop. Just as well, Richard decided; he was beginning to worry about the condition of his mare; her breathing was becoming laboured. She had gone gallantly and galloped far. He should not ask her to do much more.

The rider in front, so far from slackening his pace, was using his heels. He had slightly altered course, and the reason soon became apparent. In one place the demesne wall had fallen, and in the gap a bank had been built, an Irish double bank, familiar to anyone who has hunted in the country but to Richard an experience as novel as it was alarming. His mare had carried him so well all day, he must not lose faith in her now. Were she content to scramble over the bank, all might be well. But if she tried to clear it in one leap . . . Fifty lengths ahead, the leading horse took off, landed close to the top, paused, and then jumped clear. How steep was the drop on the far side? Richard would know in a few seconds. Once again he leaned forward and grasped the mane, felt the familiar shudder in her loins as the mare gathered herself to spring . . .

It was quite dark. Where was he? And where had everybody gone? Comfortably stretched out on what his fingers decided was moss spread with autumn leaves, he was wary of making any movement that might discover some injury to his limbs. As if looking for the answer to some intellectual game, he began to piece his recent experiences together. His mare? Where was she? And what had put him down there? As he remembered the picture of a horse leaping off the top of a bank, he looked up and saw what was shutting out the light – from where he lay it could have been the face of a mountain.

His own face was hurting him. Gingerly, he put up fingers and they came away wet. Blood, he realized, when he looked at them. Then, with elaborate cimcumspection, he clambered to his feet. His head, in contrast to his limbs, felt marvellously light. Nothing about him felt as if it was broken; but when he started to walk the left leg gave the impression of having set up in business on its own account.

He was in a clearing in a wood, made presumably for

the benefit of the enthusiast who built the double bank. It
was a short distance to the avenue, and out of the trees
the light was better. The sun had asserted itself defiantly
at its going down, and there was an angry glow in the
western sky, wholly appropriate as a background to the
ruins of Ballyorney. That he should be in the Templeton
demesne was not a complete surprise. He had thought of
the possibility when he saw he was approaching some
great house. There were not so many in that part of the
country. What did astonish him – for all the lightness of
his head – was to see that the mansion was no longer in
ruins. The lower rooms were lit up; shining through the
fanlight, the hall lamps made a decorative pattern on the
gravel sweep. There were lights in some of the rooms
upstairs. They beckoned to him. The house seemed to be
inviting him in.

The front door stood open; the hall, he noticed, was lit
by gas; there was nobody to be seen, but through a door
immediately in front of him came the comfortable rumble
of voices and occasional laughter. When he opened the
door, five candle-lit faces turned to see who was interrupting their dinner. He recognized every one of them – three
girls in very low dresses, all rather alike, and at each end
of the table their parents, looking old in early middle age.
The man, in particular, was as familiar as an old friend.
Richard knew those features much better than his own
father's; and it seemed inevitable and natural when he
rose from the table and came forward with hands outstretched. 'Richard, my dear boy. You have come back
after all.'

Before their father could get to him the girls had fallen
on Richard like house spaniels. Then one of them
shrieked, 'Oh, his poor face, is bleeding.' And there
followed an interval while the scratches were being min-
istered to. While this was going on, the girls' mother, as

insubstantial as the numerous veils and ribbons that adorned her person, pressed Richard's face against her thin bosom, murmuring incoherently and suffocating him with the scent of patchouli.

'Look to your mother, Lucy. This has been too much for her. Catherine, you had better lie down. Girls, help your mother up to bed.'

Lord Templeton's agitation was extreme; and, certainly, Richard had never seen (except in an old daguerreotype his mother treasured) a face making so fragile a frame for the sad eyes that filled it.

'Now, Catherine, my dear, up you go. Richard will come and talk to you by and by,' her husband assured her as she looked back longingly when her daughters were hustling her away.

'I'm afraid you must find your mother sadly failed,' Lord Templeton said as he shepherded Richard to the table where an extra place had been laid for him. The servant in livery behind his chair said, 'We are all delighted to see you back safe, Mr Richard, sir.' Only when he tried to sit down did Richard become aware of his injured leg. It had to be manoeuvred into position.

'Eat up your soup. We were waiting for the main course, but I dare say there will be some confusion in the kitchen at the great news. Have you told them, Rooney?'

'Yes, my lord. Nancy had hysterics, but Mrs Evans threw a bucket of cold water over her. Everyone is delighted that Mr Richard is safe and well.'

Richard was guiltily conscious of his host's scrutiny. 'Tell me how you got here,' he blurted out at last, 'and why are you in riding clothes? And why, my dear boy, did you not think of sending a telegram to tell us you were on your way? You haven't changed, I fear. When the gardener's boy came in this morning, roaring his head off – MISTER RICHARD'S COME HOME – I thought your mother was going to faint. We hadn't heard a word from you since your letter came from Varna, and that was months ago. And then, when the household was congregated on the steps to greet you, and you never appeared, I can't tell you how cast down we all were, the women particularly. I felt like strangling the wretched boy with my own hands, but the poor little fellow looked more woebegone than any of us and nothing would shake him. He swore on the Bible and stuck to his story, that he had seen you in riding clothes, leaning on the paddock fence. You didn't look up or seem to notice him, so he ran ahead with the good tidings. What happened to you? Where did you hide yourself? When we were trying to get the truth out of the boy he let out that you looked very sad, which was hardly a compliment to the family.'

'I've had a very bad fall, sir. My head feels very light. Could we postpone this talk for the present?'

'By all means. The main thing is that you are home and safe. I can't attempt to describe how your mother has worried over you. The electric telegraph is a marvellous invention; but I wonder are we ready for it. In my view it brings the war very close to home. And on top of our other troubles – the way that elder brother of yours is going on, spending his entire life, it seems, in Paris – Lucy comes begging us to let her go out to the Crimea as a nurse. She may think better of that now that you are home again. Well, girls, how is your mother?' He broke off as the three sisters came in and sat down in their places.

'Quite comfortable,' the eldest said. 'But I think it would be kind of Richard to go to her as soon as he can. I think she ought to get as much sleep as possible.'

'Richard will go when he has finished his dinner. I'm broaching the last bottle of my grandfather's claret. It will be ready when you come down. Dick, you old rascal, I was waiting for the day.'

Lady Templeton's condition kept the girls talking while Richard laid in to a succession of dishes, aided by a claret excellent in its way, but only a curtain-raiser to the entertainment to come.

'Tell me candidly, do you notice a great change in her?' the eldest girl inquired when she had an opportunity to talk to Richard by himself.

'She does look very frail,' he said. He could hear himself, and he sounded genuinely concerned. He was too interested in the scene to question his own sincerity. He was in the play and watching the play, wholly absorbed by his two rôles. Now Lord Templeton was inviting his confidence, lowering his voice so that it increased its penetrative power, and was audible in every corner of the room.

'I have misgivings about Dr Perry's treatment. Bleeding is all very well for my troubles. But for a delicate woman, suffering from chronic anaemia, does it seem sensible to be drawing blood regularly? I don't think so. Perry is a great improvement on his predecessor. Quite gentlemanly, and scrupulously clean in his person, not like that other sawbones, who may have been clever, but I couldn't stand the idea of his putting his filthy paws on your mother. But I wish I had faith in Perry's remedies. He certainly succeeds in keeping her quiet. She doesn't fuss anything like she used to.'

One of the girls – Caroline – impatient at being kept out of the male conversation, raised the question of Richard's erratic behaviour. She wanted to know where he had been all day. The park had been scoured in the search. Papa had driven into the village to make inquiries and had gone all the way to the station to ask if his son had travelled down on the morning train. 'I know what you did, you naughty boy. You couldn't delay even to see your poor sisters. Nothing would do you but to go out with the Harriers before you had even passed your family the time of day. And we hadn't seen you for more than two years. Admit it, you wretch. You could talk about nothing in your letters to me except to inquire how the building of the double bank was going on. There were times when I was so infuriated I said it would be the price of you if you broke your neck the very first time you tried to jump over it.'

'Caroline! What a horrible, horrible, thing to say,' her sisters exclaimed in chorus.

'I'm sorry,' Caroline wailed, and began to cry in earnest.

'They are all upset,' their father explained to Richard. 'You know how it is with women.'

There was a general anxiety to get Richard up to the sick woman's room as soon as possible. When the girls rose from the table, Caroline came very close to him and whispered, 'I've promised Edward.' Before Richard could think of a reply, she was following her sisters out of the room. At the door, she turned and put a finger to her lips.

'I'll be waiting for you here. We can stretch our legs out in comfort and enjoy our wine,' Lord Templeton said when Richard left him alone with the precious bottle. He was not looking forward to the tête-à-tête upstairs.

The hall was empty; and it was only when he became aware of this – he had expected to find himself in a flutter of girls – that he realized he had no clue to help him to find Lady Templeton's rooms. The stairs led on to a landing on which there were six doors. Four, presumably, of the principal bedrooms; the other two gave, respectively, on to a passage containing other rooms and a smaller staircase leading to the upper floor. Richard knocked on all the four closed doors, once, gently, on each; and, when no answer came, loudly. There was something exasperating in the absurdity of the situation.

Without much conviction, he went the length of the passage, knocking, as he passed, on each door, not expecting to hear a voice, and not hearing one. Defiantly, he opened the last door and stepped into darkness. A mouse ran across his feet and scuttled into the wainscot. When his eyes became accustomed to the dark he saw that the room was empty. There was no carpet on the floor; the window was shuttered. On returning to the landing, he went up to the first of the four doors, and turned the handle. The full moon stared at him through a hole in the wall. He looked down where the floor should have been and saw a pit. When he stepped back, the door slammed. He stood, waiting for his heart to resume its normal beating, then dragged himself across the landing to the banisters, and used the rail to support a series of kangaroo hops on his working leg down the stairs. There was no light in the hall, and when he opened the dining-room door, where he expected to see Lord Templeton glowing in candlelight, the room was deserted. And someone had removed the furniture. The hall door stood open.

He came out of the dark and was relieved to see all the candles lit in Heaven. He went out through the open door and as before followed the course of the avenue without being conscious of making any decision in the matter. Had his body felt as light as his head, he would not have been surprised to find himself wafted down the drive and over the iron gate at its prosaic end. But he was attached to a deadly weight in his injured leg. He had to drag it along; and his progress was as slow as a snail's. Once he halted and looked back at the house where, a few hours earlier, he had met with so loving a welcome. It had vanished. The black outline of the roofless pile that had taken its place seemed to threaten him. He turned away, but the menace of that transformation cast its shadow over the moon's delight. The magic of the evening had fled, and the stars, when he looked up at them, were as hard as diamonds. They danced, but not for him. He was alone in the night. Or not alone; for he was suddenly gripped by a fear that had been gradually building inside him since he went to look for Lady Templeton. In the distraction of his recent visit he had forgotten the hunt and the devilish rider who had led him into this adventure. No decent member of the Hunt would have let him lie at the bottom of a ditch or allowed his horse to run loose. The wooden-faced girl groom must have been distracted by his failure to report. He was sorry for that.

The genial spell had been rudely broken. There was evil abroad. It leered from the skeleton of the ruined house; it was following him. He was certain of its presence. Behind him? How close? He dared not look back. His spine froze under the intensity of its concentrated malevolence. He tried to go faster, but the effort resulted in a stab of pain in his groin, so exquisite that he threw his head back involuntarily. There was nothing there. Nobody. He could see down the avenue as far as the house and across the fields where patient cattle stood waiting for the dawn to break. He was not threatened by anyone. The silence of the night which had been absolute until then – he knew when a bird moved on its branch from the rustle of a leaf – was shattered by his sudden laughter. It rang across the sleeping fields and echoed in the distant hills. He looked up at the stars; they too were dancing with relief, and now, at last, he was coming close to the trees at the lodge gate. From under their shadow the avenue ran like a ribbon in a bride's hair until it arrived at his feet. He liked that image as it occurred to him, and the soft shadows, after the garishness of the sky, had a peacefulness, a mystery (becoming to a bride). They lay all about the end of the bright path, deepest under the wych elm which hid the lodge from view – the lodge in which his mother was born fifty-five years ago.

The shadows, perturbed by the moon's indecent display, were whispering to themselves, coming gently together for comfort, or stealing shyly away. One he saw distinctly move from the darkest corner and creep into the moon's path where it lay like a dark pool until it came forward, assuming a more emphatic shape. A ship. No. A horse. A horse with a man in the saddle. The illusion was complete until the shadow moved back and merged in the others.

Richard was concentrating so hard on pulling his bad leg along that he had never thought to ask himself what was to happen when he did arrive at the gate, how he was going to scale it, where he intended to go after that. Very soon these questions would force themselves on his attention. Meanwhile . . . He looked up and was startled to see how the shadows had lost their opacity. The lodge was quite plainly to be seen and, beside it, as if on guard, a man on horseback. He must have had Richard under surveillance for the whole of his slow, painful journey. If so, he gave no sign. Richard was not taken in by that. He recognized him at once. That arrogant carriage of the head . . . There was going to be a confrontation now, and Richard welcomed it. He was no longer afraid. His ghosts were laid. Nothing human could frighten him.

The rider moved his horse away from the lodge, bringing it into the full light of the moon. The effect was dramatic. Richard took note of two things: the rider was wearing the uniform of a cavalry officer, with a rent in the tunic where it was discoloured by a recent stain; and only one foot was in the stirrups, the other hung limply by the horse's side. The other thing that Richard noticed was the horse. It was not the one that the stranger had ridden in the hunt. He was seated on Richard's mare.

He suffered Richard's stare without any show of resentment; but, when the examination was completed, rode slowly back towards the trees, pausing to raise a hand in salute. There was no trace of his former insolence in the gesture, and a brother could not have looked on Richard more gently. It was difficult to believe that this soldier and the afternoon's devil were the same person. In trying to reconcile these opposites, Richard was suddenly assailed by an irresistible longing to look once more into the stranger's appraising eyes, for he was convinced that if he were to he would see his own reflected there. He tried to call out, but no sound came from his throat; tried to run forward, but his injured leg allowed no escape. Richard had a question to put to him, a question that would haunt him to the edge of the grave if he did not get the answer now.

When he arrived at the lodge, the soldier was nowhere to be seen; but the mare was peacefully cropping the short grass under the trees, and looking none the worse for her adventures.